Lunchtime Chronicles:

Carolina Reaper

By Keta Kendric

Messy Mandy Presents:
The Lunchtime Chronicles Season 3
Carolina Reaper

Cover art by Wicked Smart Designs
Pexels cover photo by Ralph Rabago
Editors: One More Glance, A.L. Barron and Tam Jernigan, publisherchick1@gmail.com

ISBN: 978-1-7332914-3-9 / Carolina Reaper

Table of Contents

Dedication

To my future Alphas. I hear you. I see you. It's only a matter of time before I write your story.

Welcome to Messy Mandy Presents:

The Lunchtime Chronicles Season 3

The Lunchtime Chronicles was launched by Author Siera London at the Interracial Author's Expo in Daytona Beach in 2019 with the novella, Whipped. The erotic romance novellas are presented like a magazine issue, lunchtime themed, and released by a diverse group of authors each season. For the latest gossip and updates from your favorite Lunchtime Chronicles authors, please follow the Facebook page: Lunchtime Dish with Messy Mandy.

Carolina Reaper Synopsis:

Zyana: One phone call flipped my life so far out of order, I ended up in the hands of a dangerous motorcycle club gunman that went by the name, 'Snake Eyes.' The man dripped sex appeal, breathed danger, and lived outside the law, and I'd be damned if I didn't want his fire to defrost my hidden desires.

Israel: When my longtime friend asked me to protect the sister I never knew he had, I volunteered with no questions asked. I assumed the job would be easy, but you know what they say about assuming. Danger was a patch I wore on my cut with pride, but nothing within my lethal arsenal could help me extinguish the fire Zyana ignited in my soul.

Warning: This novella is an interracial romance that contains strong violence, explicit sexual content, and is intended for adults.

The **Carolina Reaper** is one of the hottest chili peppers in the world. Ingesting the reaper can leave a person in serious discomfort for a day or two as they process the capsaicin. Developed by: South Carolina breeder, Ed Currie. Origin: Fort Mill, South Carolina. Hybrid parentage: Ghost Pepper x Habanero. Scientific name: Capsicum chinense 'Carolina Reaper.'

CHAPTER ONE

Zyana

The voice of the man sitting across the table from me was nothing but a lingering echo of sound that buzzed like an irritating fly at my ear. He bragged about his extraordinary job in the medical field, his doctor mother, and judge father. The boastful words he spoke of his personal life were lost on me and just as endless as the chatter of the other diners in the restaurant we sat in.

This was the fifth man I had plucked from the N2U dating app that boasted an eighty percent success rate of adequately assessing your compatibility. The app was rated one of the best on the market, so I was starting to accept that maybe I was the problem.

My decision to jump back into the shark-infested waters of the dating pool had me attempting to figure out why I had been so fascinated with the rituals of dating in the first place. Where there was once excitement and anticipation, I could now sit through a date for hours as unenthused as if I were home watching mindless television.

Dating was an unrehearsed performance. Show the other person your best behavior before you gradually let them see who you truly were. When your ex-boyfriend had attempted to pimp you out to a high-profile drug kingpin in an effort to gain a new supplier, you were more inclined to want to know your date's intentions upfront.

"So, Brandon, you say that you're a physician's assistant?" I asked, pleased that I had remembered his name. My question launched him into a monologue about his accomplishments, goals, and dreams. I'd shared mine with him in one sentence. *"I'm an ambitious hairstylist who has plans to own my own salon within the next three years."*

I sighed. Where the hell were the men who weren't afraid to show you who they really were and left it up to you to decide if you wanted to deal with them?

Candles flickered, and soft music whispered as my gaze roamed the dining area that set the stage for romance, a foreign concept because it no longer held the fiery appeal I once craved. Bored, I speared a piece of my crab-stuffed lobster tail with my fork and popped it into my mouth. I nodded, not at the sound of spoken words, but at the sight of Brandon's raised eyebrows before sipping the too-sweet white wine.

My phone vibrated, breaking into the feigned interest I'd cast in Brandon's direction. A quick finger swipe showed that I had missed a call from my brother, Major. The phone came alive in my hand before I could return it to my purse, my brother calling me back.

"Excuse me, Brandon," I said, cutting into his rant about…something. "If you don't mind, I'd like to take this call from my brother."

"Sure," he replied, but his strained gaze said differently since I was apparently breaking into the conversation he'd been having with himself. I eased from our booth, my butt sliding across the leather before I headed towards the restrooms in the back of the restaurant.

I dialed while walking, then pressed the phone to my ear when it started to ring.

"Zyana," Major called into the phone after the second ring. The tension in his tone spelled trouble, causing my heart to double-time in my chest.

"What's wrong?" I stood near a table displaying a large floral arrangement right outside the door to the ladies' room.

"Your identity was leaked in a case I'm working. My cover's been blown, and the leader of the group I infiltrated knows that you're my sister. They just tried to come for me, so I can't protect you without leading them to you."

A breathless, "What?" was all I managed to spit out. I knew my brother, and if someone had come for him, and he'd caught them, they were more than likely dead or waiting to be tortured.

"Are you okay? Safe?" I asked, my leg jumping at a rapid pace as my eyes rocked in my head, scanning every direction.

"I'm good," he answered before an unnerving silence followed and urged me to check and make sure the call hadn't dropped. The background static on his end sounded before his voice returned. "I'm going to ask you a question. Answer with a yes or no."

"Okay," I replied, my voice already cracking as fear sliced through my belly.

"Are you home?" he asked.

"No."

"Good. I'm going to track where your phone is pinging and send a friend to protect you until I clean up this mess. Don't return to your house. Wait where you are, and he will meet you there. His name is Israel Sylas, and he is one of *the few* people I trust."

"Okay," I answered, failing miserably at grasping a hold of the calm I attempted to summon.

"I've got your location," Major said with a triumphant spark in his tone. "Sis, when I hang up, I need you to power off your phone and remove the battery and SIM card. Flush the SIM down the nearest toilet and toss the phone and battery in the trash. I'll get you a new one with all of your old settings."

Another long pause followed while I stood, breathing through my heart because it was in my mouth.

"I love you, sis." The caring conviction in his tone overrode my fear and melted my heart enough for it to fall back into my chest.

"I love you too," I replied before the deafening sound of the dial tone screamed in my ear. The phone became a weight in my trembling hand as my empty stare remained on the black screen, stunned by the blow my brother had just delivered.

My brother's job as an undercover cop was always my greatest source of stress. He had decided to go into law enforcement after our father was murdered ten years ago. When nothing was being done to solve our father's homicide, Major decided he would do it himself.

He had made detective in record time. His need to solve our father's murder was his motivator, and criminal justice became his life. He'd dived into law enforcement after having graduated at the top of his class with a degree in engineering and landing a great six-figure job. However, once his heart was set on finding our father's killer, nothing stood in his way. Not a degree, or job, or a woman.

I flipped my phone in my hand and popped the back off. My nail slid under and picked at the small piece of plastic until I was able to slide the SIM card free of the metal housing that held it in place.

I turned my shoulder into the bathroom door and shoved it open before stepping into one of the stalls and flushing the SIM. The metal trash bin filled with discarded paper towels swallowed my phone and battery after I shoved them deep inside.

A glance in the mirror showed my eyes were already bloodshot, not with tears, but from the biting fear that turned my body into one big pounding heartbeat. Major was good at keeping the dangers of his job away from me as there had only previously been one other scare like this that he had taken care of within a few days. However, I got the impression that this time was different.

The criminals he hunted were willing to use anything against him if his cover was blown, and I was the easiest target. Aside from my aunts, uncles, and cousins, who we visited on occasion throughout the year, it was just Major and me. He was thirty-two, older than me by six years, and he slung his authority around enough for me to see him as my brother and a father figure.

Shit! Why hadn't I thought to call my friends and leave a message on the answering service at work before I tossed my phone? If I missed my scheduled hair appointments, the salon would call, and if my friends didn't hear from me, they would go to my apartment looking for me.

Now, I had to go back out there and finish pretending to like Brandon with all this shit on my mind. Was Major going to be okay? Were the people he had gotten involved with already at my house?

"Are you okay?" Brandon asked after I returned to the table and plopped down in my seat. The warmth on my cheeks told me they were flushed, but my pecan brown skin tone in the dim light of the restaurant would help to conceal my distress.

"I'm fine," I lied, inhaling deeply.

Satisfied with my reply, Brandon continued where he had left off before I had stepped away from the table. His incessant rambling was exactly what I needed to pass the time, and the flash of fake interest I showed apparently pleased him.

My attention was being drawn to the large darkly-tinted windows that gave me a dim view of the restaurant's parking lot. Nothing appeared out of place, as people milled about, entering and exiting the place and climbing into and out of cars.

My gaze locked on a big white guy, dressed head to toe in black, rolling through the parking lot on a black motorcycle. My first thought at the sight of him was: *outlaw*. Thankfully, he exited the parking lot, and although the man had nothing to do with my situation, I breathed a sigh of relief.

"You seem distracted. Would you like more wine?" Brandon asked, already topping off my glass. If he thought he was liquoring me up to take me home, he was better off getting the waitresses' number.

My eyes bucked, staring at that parking lot with a string of horrific scenes playing out in my mind. I'd already slipped my purse around my body in case I had to run. My gaze fell on Brandon, hoping he had good enough sense to follow if he saw me running.

Needing something to take the edge off, I picked up the glass of wine and sipped. Where the hell was this friend my brother was sending?

CHAPTER TWO

Israel

After circling the parking lot of the restaurant that Major had informed me his sister would be, I finally spotted her gray Nissan Maxima parked in a dark corner along the side of the building. Night had descended fast, and although the parking lot remained busy with customers coming and going, the dangerous crew that Major had gotten mixed up with was the kind that didn't care about collateral damage.

Zyana Mckee was a secret Major had kept well. The fact that she was right here in Charleston proved how serious he was about protecting her identity. I'd known the man for ten years and never knew he even had a sister until he called in this favor an hour ago.

He had requested that I take her with me if necessary. A request like that from Major meant that he had already separated someone's soul from their body. I memorized the photo he sent me to identify his sister before deleting it as he had requested.

Based on the picture, she was cute, and her prize-winning smile hinted at a nice, inviting personality, the opposite of her brother's. Major had the characteristics of a diamondback rattlesnake, and like me, he was meaner than a motherfucker, which was why we got along.

After I parked my Harley in the parking lot of the Lavish Comforts Hotel, I hiked next door and marched into the Elite Feast Restaurant like I owned the place. My appearance and menacing stare guaranteed funny looks, so there was no reason for me to be all happy-go-lucky.

The scruff on my face, the ominous glare I wore with honor, and the black leather cut of my motorcycle club draped on my back made me a suspect in most eyes. Finishing off the look with a long-sleeved black shirt, jeans, and boots ensured that the only people who considered me normal were members of my MC.

My mind was set on finding Zyana and getting the fuck out of this restaurant before trouble came knocking. Body coiled and ready to strike, and my gaze fixed with hell's fury shining in its fiery depths—this restaurant's untimely demise was on the horizon if anyone stepped to me.

"Sir! Sir! You need to check-in to be seated," the pansy-ass host called out before bringing a walkie up to his mouth. There was no need for him to call security because I'd already tied up the two guards, with their snoozing-on-the-job asses and left them hanging out in the dumpster with the rats. I marched past the host, fully capable of seating myself wherever the fuck I wanted.

The moment my gaze connected with Zyana, I was stopped in my determined tracks. *What the fuck?* This was a breathtaking first. She possessed that *it* thing that some women spent major money attempting to achieve.

Three spaces down and across the aisle, I stood behind a booth, facing her. Her picture was nothing but a dull replica to the true depth of the live version. She was a living intoxication that had me instantly drunk.

Instead of approaching right away, I took her in, allowing my gaze to fall over her smooth skin tone that glowed like dark honey despite the dim lighting. Her eyes were opaque brown or maybe even black from what I could tell, but they shone with a brightness that put them in competition with the sparkle on her vibrant skin.

Her hair was styled in a layered bob that brushed her shoulders and held that fashionable quality that was worthy of a magazine cover. My observation paused on her mouth because the sight of those lips, so lush and sensual, had my dick taking the lead on my thinking.

The table hid most of her body, but there was no need to see the rest of her to know that this woman was trouble. The kind of complicated trouble that would have me tying my dick in a knot and putting a muzzle on my mouth to keep my tongue out of her pussy. Fuck it, I may have to handcuff myself to my motorcycle and swallow the key because she had every part of me itching for a taste, a touch, a sniff.

Stamping down the raging need that had surfaced, it was time to introduce myself before the waitress heading my way stopped to ask me to place an order. I strolled up to Zyana and her date's table and nudged the talking bastard with a hard shoulder shove before sliding into the booth next to him.

"Who the hell are you? You have the wrong table, pal," he stated, turning in the seat to look upside my head. Dollars to doughnuts, he wasn't going to do shit but run his mouth.

Focusing on Zyana, I reached a hand across the table, preparing to introduce myself. She jerked back and sat blinking at my offered hand like it was the wide-open mouth of a snake.

"Excuse me. You need to leave. Waitress!" the talker next to me shouted, cutting off my introduction. Though reluctant, I dragged my gaze away from Zyana and glared at her date.

"Get out of our—" A quick upward jab, delivered to his weak ass jaw, shut him the fuck up while Zyana released a scream that was muffled by her hands cupping her wide mouth. Her date slumped in my direction, and my hard shove sent his sleeping ass against the wall of the booth before he tumbled head-first into his plate of food.

Zyana shot out of the booth and took off in a mad dash. "Help!" she screamed her way to the front of the restaurant. Her clumpy steps sounded as she attempted to run in heels and that cute little blue dress she wore.

"He's back there. He punched out my date. You have to call the police," she told the wait crew who were gathered near the bar area.

"He's coming!" she yelled, darting behind the bar with the rest of the group. At the sight of me, diners and the staff visibly cringed and ducked out of my way, unwilling to test the way I looked with the way they presumed I would act.

Six-foot four inches and two-hundred and fifty pounds of suspected killer is what people saw, and I preferred it that way. It meant I rarely got fucked with.

Once I was at the bar, I leaned across it, making the three staff members and Zyana hustle back. "Zyana, I'm—"

"You leave her alone! I'm calling the police on you," the woman on the phone with the apron tied around her waist yelled in my direction.

"Zyana. You need to come with me." My words were mingling with those of her protectors yelling for me to stay away. *Fuck!* I didn't have time for this shit.

At this point, the whole place had gone still, leaving the music pouring in from hidden speakers to beat at the piercing silence. The voice of the 911 operator sounded, giving the woman on the phone instructions.

My stalking approach made them all shuffle away as a group while I made my way to the opening that led behind the bar. The one holding the phone was too slow, so I yanked the phone from her hand and tossed it in the trash bin behind the bar.

The two young males standing in front of Zyana had balls as they were willing to get their asses beat to protect a perfect stranger. However, this was their lucky night because she didn't have plans to wait for me to make my next move. She was climbing up and across the counter. The heels and dress were giving her hell, but she hopped over and took off for the front door.

"Shit!" The last place she needed to be was alone and in that dark parking lot.

"Zyana!" I yelled after her while making a beeline for the front door, barely catching her retreating back as she exited. Wide eyes shined at me from every direction inside the dim space of the restaurant. Some lifted phones as they attempted to record and snap pictures of the dim scene.

Once out of the front door, I spotted her running into the darkness. She had run out of the heels and left them lying in the middle of the parking lot. I had to give her credit. If I were the bad guy, she was not going to be taken easily.

Her keys hitting the pavement sounded as I made out her shadowy figure hunched near the back of her car.

"Come on. Fuck." Her curse words registered. Once she had the keys, the lights on her car flashed, signifying she had disarmed it.

The blinding light of an approaching car came barreling around the back of the dark building, which urged me to pick up the pace of my run. My seasoned eye caught the sight of a pistol before I gripped Zyana's arm and pulled her down to the ground.

Tap! Tap! Tap!

Bullets pounded into the back of her car. The shooter's weapons were silenced, so the punching impact of the bullets merged with her ear-splitting screams. She fought my tight grip while I dragged her to the front of the car and clamped a hand over her mouth once we were in place.

"I'm here to help you, woman. Calm the fuck down. I'm Israel Sylas. Major sent me."

At those words, she calmed but continued her attempts to squirm out of the cage of my arms. That is until more bullets pounded into her car, and the sound of her back window shattering stilled her.

"I need to return fire, or they're going to keep shooting until you're dead. Can I have my hands back?" I asked but didn't let go until she nodded.

I dropped my hands to pull my pistol from my waistband and took up a prone position on the ground. Zyana jerked away and scrambled back on her butt, revealing that she still didn't trust me. The men climbed out of their vehicle, leaving it running with the doors open after pulling to a stop behind Zyana's car.

"Zyana. Lie face down and slide as far under your car as you can get," I ordered.

Thankfully, she didn't protest because the moon provided just enough illumination for me to make out the two men approaching, but it also made us targets. As soon as a sliver of light revealed enough of one within my kill range, I centered my aim between his eyes and let my finger flex against the trigger.

The silencer on my pistol didn't tell any secrets, but the man's body hitting the ground told me all I needed to know. The quick steps of his buddy sounded behind me, causing me to flip and fire, but he didn't fall. My bullet had disoriented him enough that he staggered back, giving me enough time to stand and deliver a clean shot to his face at point-blank range.

The power of the shot punched through the top of his head and sent brain matter flying out the back of his skull. His body teetered back and forth before it decided to tilt in my direction. He hit the ground face-first with a hard flesh-smacking thump, landing parallel to where Zyana had slid under the front of her car.

"Oh my God!" she screamed, letting me know she'd been introduced to the asshole who had come for her.

"We have to go. They are going to send more guys after you." I spoke while gripping the dead man's pants legs and dragging him out of the way so that she could slide from under the car.

"How do I know *you're* not the bad guy?" she questioned while dusting herself off and backing cautiously away from me.

"Your brother, Major, sent me to help you," I told her, moving every time she moved in case she attempted to run.

"How do you know my brother?" she asked like she was planning to do an interview. She kept glancing at the gun in my hand, the dead man at our feet, and her open car door.

"Look. I don't have time for this. Unless you want to be picking bullets out of your ass, I suggest you stay with me."

"Or what?" she asked.

She ran for her car door, snatching it open wider and attempted to climb in. I gripped her in a tight bear hug from behind, which caused her to release a loud scream that was stopped when I clamped my hand over her mouth. The hammering of the heel of her foot came next, inflicting damage to my shins.

"We can do this the easy way or the hard way. I'm going to let go, and you're going to be a good little girl and stop that fucking yelling. Right?" My teasing tone probably didn't help matters, but I couldn't help myself with this feisty little ball of hellfire.

She nodded and mumbled, "Um hum," before I dropped my hand.

"Why can't I follow you in my car if you're who you say you are?"

"First, you're boxed in." The gunmen's car was still running behind hers, and a cement privacy wall was about six feet in front of her car, separating the hotel's lot from the restaurant. "Second, I know you know that your brother does not hunt down run-of-the-mill criminals. If they know where you are, they already have your license plate. Now, let's go," I barked in my most commanding voice.

Apparently, my voice had no effect on this hardheaded-ass woman because she went right back to screaming.

"Help! Somebody help me!"

I picked her up and tossed her screaming over my shoulder. The sound of sirens no less than three minutes out was as troubling as the sound of the crowd gathering at the side of the building.

People gawked and pointed at my dark figure strolling through the parking lot with a woman tossed across my shoulder, kicking and beating the shit out of my back. Thankfully, the crowd hadn't spotted the dead men in the darkness.

I turned us away from the crowd and headed deeper into the dark to the opening that would get me back into the hotel's parking lot. Once we reached my bike, I set Zyana in place on the back with a hard thud and yanked her legs apart so she would straddle the seat.

"I have a damn dress on, you fucking psychopath," she spat while yanking her dress down those sexy ass legs of hers. "And no shoes, you crazy fool. You can't expect me to ride on this thing like this," she continued to spit her words while I tossed my leg across the seat and climbed on, crowding her space and wedging myself between her legs. My closeness shut her the hell up.

"I promised your brother that I'd protect you, so even if I have to tie your hard-headed ass to me to keep you alive, that's what I am going to do."

Reaching down, I gripped her ankles and drew her flush against my body, making her gasp and beat at my back as she called me every word that sounded best with the word, *fucking*. When I sat her feet atop my thighs, she snatched them back down.

Massaging my throbbing temples and taking deep breaths did nothing to douse my burning irritation. I shot a sharp glare over my shoulder that at least stopped her from hitting me in the back.

"If you don't put your legs up, the exhaust pipe is going to burn the shit out of you, and I'm not stopping while your skin is melting because there will probably be bullets flying at your fucking back. You need to stay seated in the position I put you in and shut the fuck up with all the unnecessary mouth action. You're giving me a fucking headache."

Finally, there was tense silence, except for the crowd on the other side of that barrier whose voices carried along the night's dark sky. I didn't address the part about Zyana hitting me because I liked it. The licks were foreplay as far as I was concerned. When I turned and placed my helmet on her head and snapped the chin strap closed, loud huffs and eye rolls were the thanks I received.

She didn't say shit when I repositioned her so that she was tightly against me with her legs at my waist and her bare feet locked into place in front of me. She was back there doing her best to slide her dress between her legs to cover herself or to put something between us. I didn't care what she was doing because I had her sexy ass wrapped around me either way.

"Hold on," I called back before I kicked the bike to life. She, of course, didn't listen. I reached back and took her hands before positioning them around me. My rough tug had her chest crushed into my back.

She'd had that purse slung around her, so that must have been the object she had wedged against my lower back where I was hoping her pussy would be. I revved the bike and tore out of the parking lot, not giving her any choice but to hold on tighter.

No less than ten minutes into the ride, the woman started yelling again. She kept a tight grip around my torso with one hand and was beating at my shoulder with the other.

"Let…off!" The wind kept distorting her words, but I could make out something about her being ready to get off. "Stop…now!"

A deep sigh didn't help my nerves that were as revved as my motorcycle's engine. She commenced caring out her protest, shaking my fucking torso and causing the bike to jerk and disturb what was supposed to be a fast, smooth ride.

I let up, slowing the bike down. Major would owe me for this one. Once I was sure we hadn't been followed, I veered into an empty parking lot of an electronics store that had closed for the night. The front of the building was secured by a single light affixed on a tall metal pole that made it resemble a snake standing high on its belly.

As soon as my bike screeched to a stop, she wiggled herself free and hopped off. She snatched off the helmet and shoved it at me. I stayed on my bike, glaring at her, and wondering where she was going with no shoes on. Finally, I reached for the helmet and watched her spin on her bare feet and take off.

"Where the hell do you think you're going?"

"I have a few places I can go and hide. This is not the first time I've had to do this. Thank you for your help." Her words were muffled since she didn't bother glancing back.

I slung my leg across my bike and tracked her down within seconds. "This might not be *your* first rodeo, but your brother's in deep with the Murda Mafia."

She froze at that deadly update, but still jerked away from my grip when I reached for her shoulder.

"Leave me alone," she barked in my direction.

"Nope, not going to happen. I gave Major my word, now I have to keep it, even if I have to tie you up and sling you across the back of my bike."

"I wish the fuck that you would. I don't give a damn how big and bad you think you are," she spat, and the daring glint in her eyes told me she meant every word. In the midst of our battle, I fought a smile. She was a feisty ball of fire, and that shit turned me on.

"Have it your way," were my last words before I gripped and spun her into my chest. With her wrists clamped tight in each of my hands, I drew her into me, the top of her hair tickling my stubbled chin.

The mean glare she aimed up at me was all hellfire and brimstone, the kind of look that was a lead-in for a good fuck session. She was no more than five-foot-five and one-forty max by my eye's measurements, but she had the balls of someone twice her size.

"Let go of me, you damn, fucking—" she barked, so upset she fumbled her curse words as her harsh breaths slapped against my chin.

"I do enjoy all the nice words you say to me. Turns me on," I continued while slapping a white zip tie on her left wrist before tugging her arms tight around my lower back. She wiggled, screamed, and kicked her ass off while I made repeated attempts to zip tie her hands together behind my back. If only she knew the tricks I could pull off with a few plastic ties. Her face was a mask of confusion, her eyes wide and searching as she struggled. "What are you…" Her question was stopped when she put more effort into her struggle.

A triumphant smile filled my face when I snapped her other wrist into the second tie that I had linked with her first bound wrist.

"What the hell are you doing? Let me go! Are you crazy? Let…me…go!" With the ties binding her to me, I dragged her stiff arms up my body, giving her a little space so that she wouldn't be face-planted in my chest.

With my arms at her back, I bent and wrapped my hands around her lush hips and lifted her off her feet so that I had her legs wrapped around my waist. She had gone limp and unwilling to help me. It didn't matter because she was the perfect amount of woman and her feistiness screamed that she needed to be manhandled.

Once she acknowledged the sexually compromising position I'd put her in, her eyes, wide and piercing, sparked with barely contained rage as she scanned up and down our connected bodies. The up-close view of the hot fury on her tight face had me fighting back a grin. The depth of her anger radiated off her body and flowed against my skin, drawing me in instead of warning me away.

I carried her back to the bike, wrapped around me like we were lovers, despite all the wiggling and cursing she was doing.

"You're nuts. Insane enough that after this is over I'll need to check myself into the nuthouse to get rid of your residual crazy."

"You either shut the hell up, or I'm going to put something in that mouth of yours to shut you up."

My comment made her fiery words shoot out faster, and she even snapped her teeth at me, nearly taking a chunk out of my chin. All she was doing was making me want her because I *loved myself* a sassy woman. Or maybe it was just *her*. Whatever it was, was turning me the fuck on like never before.

I lifted her higher to tuck her legs more securely around my waist, loving the way her ass and hips filled my hands. She cursed with the roaring intensity of a runaway train, and the proximity was like taking a hammer to my eardrums.

"Let me the fuck down, you fucking psycho!"

Thank fuck that damn purse of hers had shifted to the rear of her body. If she moved now, it meant she'd be rubbing her pussy against the bulge that I proudly presented to her.

The moment she felt me, she went still and her eyes locked on mine. Nothing could keep the satisfied smirk off my face. Ten inches of hard dick barely contained in my jeans had calmed her feisty ass down substantially.

"Will you at *least* cover my legs, you sick son of a bitch," she spat at me, rolling her eyes with such firm intensity, it may as well have been a slap. I untucked the leather tails of my vest and let the material fall over her exposed hips. With a solid hold of her delicious thighs, I lifted her higher and climbed across the bike, sitting her ass on the seat before me. The swift movement had caused her to lock her legs tighter around my waist and her face to radiate her fury.

"You got something else you need to say?" I asked, meeting her heated gaze. I tilted my head to glance into eyes that glowed with such burning anger it was a wonder I hadn't caught fire.

Lips poked out, chest heaving, and body shaking, I'm sure if she could have, she would have killed me. She strained against me, attempting to yank her hands free, but her movement did nothing more than make the front of her body work against mine.

"Let me fucking go," she gritted.

"Or what?" I asked. She didn't answer. "Your brother sent me to help because he's in danger too." At that update, she clamped her lips shut, and some of the tension eased from her body, but she didn't stop her attempts to wiggle free. If she kept that shit up, one of us was going to end up coming.

"As much as I know you would like to get away from me, I can't let you out of my sight until Major gives me the okay."

I kicked the bike to a roaring start that jostled her body and added to my enjoyment of her heat rubbing against mine. Releasing the grip I had on her waist, I placed my hand on her lower back and pulled her in, crushing her pelvis against mine.

My actions had her staring up wide-eyed, but she didn't say a thing about my dick, which was as hard as a crowbar and pressing into the sweltering heat she released. I revved the engine and took off in a roaring dash, which sent her slamming against me.

What should have been a ten-minute drive turned into twenty minutes, partly me making sure we weren't being followed and partly me enjoying the scorching heat of our sexy position. Based on how hot her sex was against mine and that lust-laden spark flashing in her eyes, she was as turned on as I was. Other than her adjusting to ease away from my raging hard-on, I hadn't heard another peep from her.

She glanced around when water started to come into view. Her attention was lured away from the sexual tension growing stronger between us when we drove along the path leading into the Charleston Harbor Marina. I hadn't missed her biting into her lip and her squirming against me despite the vibrating core of the motorcycle beneath us.

The tense set of her hunched shoulders, and her searching gaze, hinted that she wanted to say something about where we were. However, her knowing that I had no qualms about gagging her if I needed her to shut up had her pinching her lips together tightly as she glanced around.

Once I drove up, parked, and cut the engine, I tucked her legs tighter around me before I stood. *Dammit!* The feel of her all warm and soft against me was fucking with my heads. I had never claimed to have a type, but after one look and one touch of Zyana, I knew that she was it. My motto had always been to fuck them once and forget them, but I got the sense that she wasn't the type to be easily forgotten.

I kept my eyes locked on hers as a distraction so that she'd remain unaware that I had pulled my knife. I reached behind my back and carefully cut the zip-ties to free her from me. She took cautious steps back, eyeing me to gage my next move.

"This way," I said, stepping away before she could start shooting that mouth off again. She followed, her light steps hesitant as she rubbed her wrist and sent her head jetting around our surroundings.

"This is where you live? I thought bikers lived in trailer parks. You know, in the poor white-trash parts of town."

I smiled, wise enough to know that she was baiting me.

"One part of that statement is true. I'm white, but I've never lived in a trailer park, and I've never been poor, or trash."

"Calling it like I see it." She shrugged. "The way you look and dress and even what you ride—you don't look like you own a boat this nice."

"Snake Eyes," she said, reading off the name painted in big blue letters against the boat's white exterior. "Is this your boat, or did you kill the owners and pirate it for yourself?"

I cast a hard stare at her over my shoulder. "It's going to take a lot more than insulting words to piss me off if that's your new tactic at getting me to release you. Now, are you going to behave, or do I need to break out the zip ties again?"

She didn't render a reply but continued to follow my march to the edge of the pier that would lead to the boat's deck and its entrance. Once I was at the door, I keyed it open and waved my hand for her to enter first.

"Unladylike first," I stated and could have sworn she smiled before strolling past me.

Once inside, I locked us in with two pressing concerns ripping my mind apart. How the hell was I going to keep her strong-willed ass from running? More importantly, how the hell was I going to keep myself from fucking her?

CHAPTER THREE

Zyana

This couldn't have been his boat. He was a dirty-looking biker. Maybe not dirty, but dangerous looking enough for me not to feel safe with him, even if my brother *did* send him. Okay, so maybe he had that hot white boy thing going for him, but it wouldn't be the first time a woman found a serial killer sexy.

Those damn arresting, light-green eyes, that tall sexy body, and his strong masculine physique made me forget I was mad. And how could I forget his dick print in those jeans? If he was packing what I thought I felt, there were some broken down vaginas in Charleston.

Focus dammit! Focus! I reprimanded myself. The man was crazy. Who in their right mind zip ties a woman to their body? Who in their right mind smashes his hard dick into a woman they've just met and think it's okay? Who in their right mind shoots people dead without a second thought?

I hadn't mentioned the bodies he'd dropped for fear that my ass would be next. Thankfully, the dark area saved me from the sight of the horrific images. How was I supposed to get in touch with my brother? Did this man even know my brother?

Now, I was alone with this homicidal lunatic, trying to focus long enough to hatch an escape plan. And the way he kept staring like he was ready to rip my clothes off had me itching to take out the small can of mace I kept in my purse, my killer-be-gone spray.

He had taken a seat, but I continued to stand, rooted in place at the front door.

"Here. Your brother wants to speak to you." I spun at the deep rumble of his voice before my gaze dropped to the phone in his hand. Three quick steps put me in front of him before I snatched it from his grip.

"Major!" I yelled, not caring that insane-in-the-membrane was ogling me.

"You okay, sis? Israel told me that you two ran into a little trouble at the restaurant." I rolled my eyes before spinning and putting my back to crazy ass.

"A little trouble?" I hissed the question at my brother in a low tone. "Do you know this guy? Why didn't you ever tell me about him if you do?" I continued questioning Major while casting a side-eye over my shoulder in Israel's direction on the couch.

"He and I are…complicated. Kind of like I never tell you details about my cases because of the danger. He's that kind of complicated."

"If he's so complicated, why the hell did you send him for me? The man's crazy. He dropped two bodies like it was nothing, and—"

The dark shadow that emerged was draped over me like it intended to swallow my soul. Israel was standing behind me; his six-foot-forever frame was looming over me like a dark angel.

"I know. He already told me he had to put two men down and zip tied you to calm you down. Please stay with him. I trust him to keep you safe."

My brother couldn't have been serious. I chanced a glance back, rolling my eyes now that I knew my tattling session with my brother wasn't going to work. When the hell did he have the opportunity to tell Major that he'd tied me up and killed men?

"Z," Major called. "I need you to stay with him until I get this shit straightened out. If something happens to you because of me—" he stopped abruptly, unwilling to allow me to hear the sadness that was dulling the strength of his tone.

Major had always taken care of me. Our mother ran off when I was two, leaving our father to raise us. After our father was murdered, Major, at twenty-two, assumed responsibility for me, and I was a handful at sixteen. He was the one who paid my beauty school tuition and my rent until I was financially stable. Therefore, if he believed putting me in the hands of a man who looked like he had served out his time on a first-degree murder charge was a good idea, I'd have to find a way to live with it.

"Okay. Be careful. I love you," I stated, my voice cracking.

"Love you too, sis," he returned before the line went dead. Without turning to face him, I handed Israel his phone across my shoulder and hugged myself after he'd taken it.

"Would you like to take a shower and get some rest? We'll head for the compound tomorrow."

I spun on my bare heels like I had wheels under my feet. "Compound?"

"Yep. My motorcycle club has its own compound. We call it Ground Zero, and it's one of the safest places in the state."

Safer for the outside world. I nodded despite my thoughts, not knowing what else to do. He lifted a hand, pointing to what I assumed were the bedrooms before he took off.

When I stepped into what I discovered was the only bedroom, Israel was handing me a small bundle of clothes. I took my time staring around, taking in the lux blue shade of the paint on the walls and soaking in the neat coziness of the room. A queen bed was draped with a stylish gold comforter and four fat, fluffy pillows. Small bedside tables with matching lamps atop them sat on either side of the bed, and a dresser that matched the gold trimming of the headboard sat along the passageway to the bathroom.

When I finally accepted the clothes, I noticed it was a new plain white T-shirt and a pair of his boxer briefs that he had thankfully taken from new packs still sitting atop the dresser.

"Thanks," I mouthed with no enthusiasm. "Where are you sleeping?" I asked.

He pointed at the bed.

"Where am I sleeping?" I questioned with a brow stuck in the air. He pointed at the same bed.

I laughed. "I'm not sleeping with you." I leaned in a little closer, with my brows pinched tight to observe him better. "You really are crazy, aren't you?"

He pursed his lips like my words did nothing but bounce off of him.

"You don't have a choice. You're a flight risk. You've tried to run twice, so now you and I must stay joined at the hip."

I cast a glance back at the living room, thinking about the comfortable-looking couch he'd been sitting on.

"The couch makes my back hurt," he stated, cutting into my thoughts. He aimed his thumb across one of his set shoulders.

"Bathroom's that way. Please be quick because the hot water doesn't last long."

I didn't render a response before I strode away and closed myself in the full-sized bathroom. There was no lock on the sliding door, so wedging something under the knob crossed my mind until my brother's voice surfaced, telling me that he trusted the guy.

After adjusting the water, I peeled my dirty and damp clothes off, realizing that they were also drenched in my sweat from the humid June air and my having to run for my life.

I jumped into the shower, allowing the spray of hot water to wash away a little of my stress. However, nothing would take away the worry I clung to for my brother's safety. I was also having trouble digesting all that had happened tonight. Unknown people had not only tracked me down, but were attempting to kill me. If Israel hadn't been there, I'd probably be dead.

The door sliding open sounded over the spray of the water, making me snap my head in the direction of the door.

"I'm not done," I called out. "Give me a few more minutes," I added when the door wasn't immediately shut.

The sound of movement inside the bathroom made my heartrate kick frantically and forced me to slide the frosty glass door open and peek out.

"What the fuck are you doing in here? I'm in the shower. Have you lost what's left of your mind?" I shouted, setting the small bathing towel in place over my lady parts, and my hand and forearm across my tits. My saucer-wide eyes were stuck staring at him.

Israel stripped off his shirt without replying or acknowledging me and proceeded to reach down and yank off his socks. My eyes bucked at the sight of all of that viral, strong...maleness.

"What the hell are you doing?" I asked, cutting into my own sick thoughts. "Get out! Are you deaf?"

"Are you deaf?" he spit the question back at me, finally glancing up. "I told you the hot water doesn't last long, and I don't feel like waiting another thirty minutes for the water to heat back up."

"What's wrong with you? How the hell are you just going to walk in on me taking a shower? Don't you have any manners? You better get your crazy ass out of this bathroom. You're not getting in here—"

My words were stopped in their tracks when he started to undo his pants. With his predatory eyes firmly set on mine, he popped the button, slid the zipper down, and sent his pants and his boxer briefs on a quick downslide.

At this point, I clutched my tits tighter and squeezed the small towel more securely against my lower parts. I jumped when the cold tile of the shower's wall kissed my back, realizing I'd been backing away from the sight of him the whole time.

When he stood fully upright, my eyes would not behave, as they went straight to his dick and locked on the thing. It wasn't even hard, and it was bigger than any I had seen. I swallowed a mix of fear and stress while my heart kicked out the erratic cadence that had started in my chest.

The man had a firm, athletic build, not ripped like a bodybuilder, but toned and strong, with a mouth-watering appeal that called to the part of my brain that conceived images of sex. Even the thin hair on his chest and happy trail below his belly button was straight sin. His delicious tan hinted that he had a flirting relationship with the sun, a light caramel that made his skin look like it would melt in your mouth.

His hair was short and wavy, no more than an inch, and the stubble on his jaw added to the sexy. And those attention-getting eyes of his. *Jesus.* The man could do anything to me right now, and my crazy ass was standing there doing a rundown of his body statistics.

Him reaching for the shower door forced me to drag my eyes away from his man-meat. Dear diary, the man was hung like someone's prize-winning stallion. I was scared to death of what he might do to me, but my tangled-up mind kept wanting to linger on what my eyes stubbornly refused to stop observing.

Unwilling to flash him by shoving him away, I shook my head and squeezed myself even deeper into the wet shower wall. The shower was large enough in area space for two, but Israel was tall, and his built body didn't leave much in the way of air or space.

Once he had stepped in, he closed the door as casually as if I weren't even there and stepped under the spray of the hot water.

"You. You." I couldn't spit out my words as I blinked rapidly at the water that splashed off his skin and dotted my face. "What are you doing?" I asked in a breathless murmur, unable to comprehend this man's bold actions.

"I'm taking a shower. I told you about the hot water, and since you insisted on staying your ass in here, this is what you get. Me in here with you."

He dipped his head under the spray and let the water wash all over his hair and run down his body with me standing at his side, watching, completely dumbstruck. My stupid ass eyes chased the water as it rained down his wide shoulders and muscled back, and farther down his tight ass and around to his dick. The bulging muscles in his powerful thighs flexed as he moved leisurely to allow the water to flow all over him.

There were tattoos everywhere. His left arm was a full sleeve, and his back, shoulders, chest, and legs all sported ink. There were cuts, knife wounds, and even what might have been a gunshot wound in his upper back, accompanied by a long vertical scar below it.

His penetrating eyes were heavy with lust when he lifted them and pinned me where I stood. Droplets of water dripped from his face, pooling along his long thick lashes as he kept those eyes on me. "There's about seven minutes of hot water left. I suggest you finish up."

He went on soaping up while I stood in place, losing my mind to shock, watching him, and waiting for the moment when he'd snap and release more crazy. He went on about his business, washing everything with ease and no shame.

I released a yelp before I jumped, banging my back into the wall when he reached up and planted his hand above my shoulder, using the leverage against the wall to reach down to wash the bottom of his legs and his feet. The positioning gave me a better view of that part of him that was now stiff, powerful, and overwhelmingly mesmerizing.

Dear Lord. The damage he could do with that thing would be irreversible. Once he was done lathering up, he repeated the rinse cycle under my probing gaze. My throat remained dry under a constant spray of water, but my eyes didn't miss the bubbles teasing their way down his body.

When he'd finished, and I was sure I was ready to pass out from the obscene mixture of fear and what I think was lust flowing through me, he stepped out. He opened a cabinet, took out a towel, and started drying off. When he was somewhat dry, he wrapped the towel around his waist and walked out.

I had no idea if I'd been holding my breath the whole time he'd been in the shower with me, but once he was out of sight, I released and sucked in air like I was learning how to breathe for the first time.

CHAPER FOUR

Israel

Ms. Loudmouth Zyana talked big shit until I got that damn heart rate of hers pumping. When I'd hopped into the shower with her, she didn't know whether to fear me or lust after me. I preferred both but figured I'd better tone it down a bit before she tried to take off on me again.

The sight of her cautious approach in my T-shirt with no bra caught and trapped my gaze. She'd pulled her damp hair into a ponytail, and those sexy brown legs against the white of my shirt probably had me looking every bit as crazy as she'd labeled me earlier.

She was one sexy ass woman with enough of everything I liked. Usually a woman had one thing and was missing another, but Zyana had it all. Nice full, *real* tits, shapely legs and thighs, and an ass plump enough to make you forget yourself. It had taken everything I had to keep from getting hard at the sight of her naked in the shower, but nothing worked, even with her hiding parts of herself from me.

Inviting her to climb into bed, I flipped the covers back and sat, waiting to see if she would continue to fight me, although, she knew I was crazy enough to take things to the extreme with her. My actions tonight must have scared the fight right out of her because she eased into bed, putting her back to me, and dragging the covers up to her neck.

I reached over and flipped the light off on my side of the bed, plunging the room into darkness. The porthole, the only semblance of a window, cast a moonlit glow into the room and enough light for me to make out her form.

"How do you know my brother?" she asked in a low tone. I smiled, glad she was getting the point that she was stuck with me. "He usually tells me everything. Well, except stuff about his cases, but he's never mentioned you."

"We've been friends for about ten years. He never told me about *you* until a few hours ago when he asked me to be your protection."

"Are you an undercover cop like him? Is that how you know him?"

"No. We had a common interest that led us to the same place."

She released a deep sigh and flipped to face me, her weight barely shifting the mattress. My eyes had adjusted enough to the darkness to make out the sexy outline of her features.

"Will you stop being cryptic and tell me how you know him? He's never going to tell me because he has the built-in big-brother gene that makes him believe he needs to protect me from everything. He thinks I don't know about the times he beat up my ex-boyfriends, or the background checks he runs on them. My ex-boyfriend Kevin treated me badly one too many times, and Major put him in the hospital and would have probably killed him if I wouldn't have asked him not to. So, please, tell me something."

The low ache of desperation in her tone made it sound like she was tired of always being left in the dark about situations.

"I belong to a motorcycle club called the Hell Reapers. Me, my brother Micah, and our oldest brother, Elijah, started running the MC after our father was killed. Elijah was voted president and me and Micah, chairmen."

She eased closer to get a better look at my face.

"Not that we expected them to do anything, but the criminal justice system didn't do much to track down our father's killer because of the perception of our MC and reputation. Even if they had done something, it wasn't going to stop us from avenging our father. Me and my brothers banded together and pooled our resources to find our father's killer. The killer turned out to be a cop."

She lifted from her pillow, her eyes growing wide against the moonlit glow in the room.

"Settle down, little lady. Your brother wasn't the cop who killed our father. Your brother and I ended up in the same place because the cop who killed *my* father was the same one that killed yours."

The revelation caused her to suck in a deep breath.

"There's not much more to tell, just that Major and I have been aces ever since. He even kept Elijah from getting a murder-one charge for homicide when we were twenty-six. Managed to get the charge down to manslaughter for six years versus the twenty-five-to-life the opposing council was going for. Micah was voted in as president when Elijah went to prison, and thanks to Major, E will be coming home in three months."

She was positioned the same as me now, on her back, with her gaze aimed at the ceiling.

"It took my brother years to admit to me that the man who killed our father was never going to prison," she said. "When he told me he'd killed him instead, I thought I'd be upset, but I wasn't even surprised. Our father was a good cop, but the cop who killed him was a member of the good-old-boys system, and sometimes, they have a way of skating through the system untouched. My brother never told me about you or your brothers, but if he gave you his word that he would never tell anyone, then that anyone included me."

She could handle more than I gave her credit for. If she knew that her brother had taken out their father's killer, then she was a lot stronger than Major was giving her credit for. We didn't speak another word afterward, and I eventually picked up on her labored breaths as she'd drifted off to sleep.

***

Zyana

So warm and fresh. And solid. And comfortable.
"Mmm," a low moan tickled my throat and lured me from the comfort of my half-conscious state. My lids fluttered open to me nuzzling my face against the warm surface of—*oh shit!*

My head was not on this man's chest. My leg was not slung across his. My pussy was not shoved up against his muscular thigh. His shirt that I wore was not lifted enough to flash him my whole damn hip. He did not have his hand wrapped around me like I had slept this way. He was not staring at me with that big ass grin on his face.

"Good morning. Sleep well?" he asked, tugging me closer to nail home the fact that I was all up on him.

It was taking a lot, and I do mean everything I had, not to jerk away from him. The big arm he had wrapped around my body was also keeping me in place.

My hand. Ole dear Lord in heaven, my hand was not on this man's junk. When he reached down and sat his hand atop the one I had sitting on his exceptionally large and ridiculously hard package, I jumped.

"I think I'm starting to understand the true reason why your brother has never introduced us. All this chemistry. We may as well stop beating around the bush and fuck already."

I jerked away after that comment, yanking my hand from under his and off his hard bulge. I shook off the weird pull his possessive craziness had on me. The man was all *levels* of insane. No filter, no chill, just shameless. All I could think was, how long is it going to take my brother to straighten out this trouble so he can rescue me from this madman?

CHAPTER FIVE

Zyana

It wasn't hard for me to admit to myself anymore that I enjoyed the way Israel felt pressed against me. His scent, a heady mix of rosewood, soap, and leather added with the way his muscles flexed against the parts of me that touched him, drew me in.

My arms were looped tight around his muscular torso and all I could think was, *Strong. Powerful. Masculine.* I was mindful not to piss him off because he didn't mind upgrading his crazy to insane. The memory of him zip-tying me and jumping into the shower with me last night flared. It was a blaring reminder of how over-the-top he could go.

Now, after making a quick stop to purchase some clothes and toiletries for me, we rode on his bike in the noon sunlight to an unknown location. The only information he gave was that the compound we were headed to was off the grid, someplace they called Ground Zero.

An hour and a half later, I was in the middle of no-
where, being led into the heart of swamp territory. We coasted
along a raised one-lane road cut between wetlands thick with
trees and natural wildlife. The road led us deeper into the
swamp where the insects chirping and buzzing grew so thick,
it acted like an extra layer of clothes.

The trees swayed on a breeze blown in off the burning
heat of the sun, hot, but flirtingly refreshing. Moisture from
the humidity didn't cling to my skin as it had the night before,
here, it merely kissed along the surface, gently reminding of
its presence. Moss hung from willowy tree branches like long
strains of wild hair that swayed lazily against the breeze.
Among the trees, the surface of the ground waved as the
unique mix of vegetation rode the lazy billowing currents of
the water beneath it.

The motorcycle decelerated as we approached a ten-
foot-high metal fence fortified by trees, vines, and the thick
foliage born of the swamp. Although I didn't have a visual of
what was behind that thick wall of vegetation and metal, I
could sense the impregnable state of the area, and feared I was
in for more insanity than I may have been able to handle.

As soon as we were within a few feet of the fence, the
metal began sliding apart so that we could enter. Instincts told
me to glance up, and when I did, I choked down a gasp as it
appeared the trees were moving in formation like the creature
from the legendary movie classic, *The Swamp Thing,* had
come to life.

The fire didn't die down on my flared-up nerves because the sun's exploring rays bounced off the metal barrel of
a big machine gun. It took me a wild-eyed moment to make
out the smiling face hidden within the camouflage outfit that

was made to blend into the surroundings. The costumed man waved and had the nerve to wink.

"Welcome back, Snake," he called down before standing to his full height.

Snake?

Another gasp escaped when two more well-camouflaged men unexpectantly moved, giving away their positions and appearing to materialize out of thin air.

One was on the ground standing next to the gate, and the others stood above us on either side of the open portion of the gate. They stood on what I could now make out as guard towers that the vegetation had naturally hidden.

We drove past the gates, and my first sight was more trees and thick undergrowth as we coasted along a narrow dirt road. The tree's wispy branches reached across the road to hug each other, providing a uniquely beautiful tunnel passage.

"You go by Snake?" I questioned Israel, peeking around his sturdy shoulder and talking over the engine's steady roar."

"Snake is short for Snake Eyes."

Like that's any better, I thought, before the name on the back of the boat flashed in my mind.

Why do you go by Snake Eyes?" I asked.

"Let's just say, when they see me, they have rolled the dice on their lives and come up snake eyes. If you're not a friend and meet these eyes—" was the unfinished answer he gave. I left that one alone. After about a half-mile, a clearing started to take shape up ahead, and I could make out buildings.

When we broke the tunneled passage, my lips parted, and my eyes feasted. I forgot all about the crazy man I was snuggled up to on the motorcycle because my attention had been snatched.

"Beautiful," I mouthed. Nature's living beauty shattered the misconception I had formed in my head about swamplands. This was like being on an island surrounded by three distinctly different natural settings.

A body of dark water sat waving on my right. The expansive stretch of land before me was a mix of woods and small patches of scattered clearings. To the left was a mix of trees and foliage so thick, I couldn't see the water I sensed hidden below the undergrowth.

The land produced fat towering trees, and the large areas of solid land presented grass so dazzlingly green, it appeared that carpet had been laid on the ground. Modern-day, well-constructed log-style cabins were spread spaciously over the area. Motorcycles appeared to be the only form of vehicles that existed within this natural metropolis.

We passed by the first cabin, big and spacious with a wraparound porch. At closer inspection, I noticed that the large opening in front gave me a view straight through the entire building as it was a pavilion where they must have had gatherings. This compound was its own small city with enough visual stimulation to have my thoughts going a mile a minute. How big was this place? Did all of this belong to the crazy man sitting in front of me?

Nearly every man we strolled past wore all black and the same black leather vest as Israel. They resembled a bunch of big, darkly-shrouded ghosts ready to hunt someone's soul. The sight of them gave life to why they were called Hell Reapers.

We rolled along at a snail's pace, which allowed me time to take in and appreciate the beauty of the area. I loved the way some of the cabins were set within the landscape, like the builders had been careful not to disturb the natural setting too much.

This place was more like a biker's retreat than a compound, as Israel had called it. Cabin after cabin breezed across my view, some sitting off the body of water and others that sat great distances away so that only the tops were visible. The deep smile on my face had yet to fall.

I'd always lived in the city, and the closest I'd come to visiting the countryside was on a few road trips with my girlfriends in college. I was so taken by the scene that it took the noise and vibration of the motorcycle stopping to break the trance.

We had parked at one of the cabins, and Israel was off the bike in a flash. He reached to help me off, casting a stern eye on me, I assumed to gage my mood. As soon as my feet touched the ground—

Boom! Boom! Boom!

The noise vibrated through the air and sounded like a giant beating his bass drums. My heart ended up in the pit of my stomach, and I didn't know whether to duck or run. The tight grip I had taken of Israel's arm wasn't lost on him or me. His gaze dropped to his watch before he glanced towards where the shots had come from. He finally let his gaze fall to meet my expectant one.

"Just the boys getting in a little target practice for the day. No need to be afraid."

That was easy for him to say. He wasn't the one being inducted into the outlaw way of life.

I hadn't let go of his arm, didn't plan to, knowing that armed men were shooting nearby. The three burly men heading in our direction didn't help my nerves either because they reminded me of escaped convicts.

"Snake," they all spoke at once, tipping their heads in our direction. Their big bodies and dusty, worn boots were enough to make the ground shake with each of their steps. Curious eyes left Israel and landed on me. Their stringent stares had me tightening my grip on Israel's arm and taking a step closer so that I was damn-near behind him. I decided then and there that I was better off with the crazy I knew.

"It's okay. I need them to see you with me. They need to know who you are *property of* so that they will not touch or even approach you."

Property of, I mouthed silently. "Did you just say that I'm your property?" I asked. The tension of being in his world was lessening because my attitude was starting to heat up.

He chuckled. "Try not to take our terms so literally. Trust me, if I claim you as my property, it keeps you safe in this world, and it will earn you a level of respect that some women have waited months, and in some cases years, to gain from us."

The tension in my face and cocked gaze kept him talking.

"When a patched member claims a woman as their property or old lady, it's as good as him marrying her. It means no other member will touch you unless they are given permission to. It also means they will protect you like you're a member of this family. There are not many women on this compound, but the ones that are, I can assure you, are happy. An unclaimed woman to us is nothing more than a piece of ass that usually gets fucked by any member that wants her. We call them CP, and we never bring them anywhere near this compound."

"CP?" I questioned with a deep dip in my forehead, fighting to understand this unique sub-world.

"Community Pussy," he replied. My eyes shot up high on my forehead. "Calling a woman your property is bad enough, but there are women who actually let you call them community pussy?"

"You have to keep in mind that we don't live by outside rules. We live by our own codes and laws. Pussy is never in short supply. The women that deal with us know our rules— some hang around when we are in town or have an event just to say that they've been fucked by a Hell Reaper."

While my brain was attempting to breakdown the lessons Israel was schooling me on, more men, who looked like they'd been sprung from hell, were walking by. They looked like they weren't opposed to skinning me and having me for dinner, and not in a sexual way either.

"You coming to church tomorrow?" one of the men called back to Israel over his shoulder. "Yeah, I'll be there," he answered the man.

Israel laughed at the obvious confusion in my expression.

"Church is our club meetings," he answered without me having to ask. The subject of me being his property popped right back to the surface.

"Is that how things work around here? You lay claim, and the rest of the members respect it?"

"I've never brought a woman home before, so your presence is a shocker. And yes, the way I'm letting you hold onto me, they know to keep their distance. The only thing I haven't done yet is patch you."

"Patch me?"

He tugged on the leather vest he wore. "To officially claim you as my property, I'll have to make you a cut similar to mine that labels you 'Property of Hell Reapers, Snake Eyes.'"

Was there a cheat sheet to this world that I could borrow? The best I could do at this point was keep an open mind and follow Israel's lead since I didn't have any other choices.

"Am I safe here?" I questioned as we walked, and more men marched by, speaking and staring.

"As long as you're with me," he replied, and I couldn't tell if it was warning or mischief sparking in his gaze.

At those words, I released the grip I had on his arm and looped my arm around his. If their MC had a strange, this-woman-is-claimed thing going on, I was willing to pretend my *ass* off as long as I wasn't left alone with any of these *killers*. I was stereotyping them, profiling—whatever, they fit the part. So did Israel, but he'd at least proven that he could be trusted not to rape and kill me.

We marched up four thick wooden steps into the cabin we had parked in front of, and the sound of heavy metal, Cemetery Gates by Pantera, stabbed at my eardrums. *A bar?* A packed one that appeared as well-stocked with people and alcohol as any I'd frequented in the city.

Billowing smoke, flying curse words, a heavy dose of testosterone, and deadly, well-built men filled the place. Israel had been right about there not being many women as the ratio appeared to be ten men to every one woman. And the women

CAROLINA REAPER · 51

that were there all wore smaller versions of the black leathered cuts that the men wore.

Were the men required to have a certain physique to be a part of this motorcycle club? It damn well appeared that way. I hadn't seen a man yet that was under six feet or less than two hundred pounds. I hadn't spotted another person of color either, which might explain why the atmosphere felt like it had frozen on the earth's rotational spin whenever eyes landed on me with Israel.

We strolled past the bar into the heart of the place to the far back wall where a poker game was taking place. The table was littered with beer bottles, sweating glasses of waiting alcohol, and big bodies huddled and concentrating on their cards.

As soon as a set of light-green eyes like Israel's landed in our direction, there was no mistaking that this was his brother.

"Snake Eyes," he called, slapping his cards on the table. His gaze raked over his brother before they latched on to me, scanning me like a laser device that could see down to the bone. I hadn't heard anyone call Israel by his given name yet, and attempting to escape the green eyes that had trapped mine was useless.

"Who's that you have with you?" the man with the intense gaze asked.

"This is Zyana, Major's sister," Israel answered. The man's face creased into a tight pinch, and I easily read the silent question he mouthed, *"Major has a sister?"*

Although no words were spoken, Israel cast a glance around the bar, causing the people to pause and acknowledge the private introduction. It appeared they'd been put in a trance spurred by a silent call I didn't understand. The music, although loud with Drowning Pool screaming, "Let the bodies hit the floor!" didn't affect the connection or the acknowledgment that was being cast around the room. There was no doubt that Israel was telling this group that I was not to be messed with as eyes traveled back and forth between him and me.

By the time I glanced back to the table, the man we'd approached had moved and was standing in front of me. His imposing height and strong build intimidated me, and I automatically clutched Israel tighter, gripping his muscled bicep with both hands.

Reluctantly, I reached for the hand the man stuck out and watched as mine was swallowed by his when he took it. "Nice to meet you, Zyana. I'm Micah, and the asshole you're with is my little brother. Since I'm the 'Pres' and beat him into this world by two minutes, I think it's only fair that I get to claim you instead of him."

Is he serious? I swallowed a thick knot of anxiety, very aware that he still hadn't let go of my hand. The loud silence that followed the comment gave me the sense that I was standing in the middle of some sort of standoff as deadly gazes collided.

The unflinching seriousness in the brother's tensed bodies and tight faces had me praying the tension would break and that I could get my hand back. The small hint of a smile Micah let peek from the corner of his lips when he sat his gaze back on mine allowed relief to pour over me.

My eyes volleyed back and forth between the brothers. Their heights and builds were similar, but they weren't identical due to Micah's dark shoulder-length hair and clean-shaven face.

"You can call me Spyder," Micah added, and the dark devilishness that flashed in his gaze sent a chill racing up my spine. When he finally released my hand and backed away, I breathed, my chest visibly rising and falling.

"Why don't you two sit and join us for lunch?" Micah offered. And like his words had the power to conjure up his demands, a woman wearing a black chef's hat and a tight, fitted black dress balanced a tray filled with a mouthwatering seafood mix piled high with mussels and crabs and corn and potatoes. The seafood boil gave off a spicy scent that instantly triggered hunger.

I sat next to Israel in the seat he'd pulled out for me, and didn't miss that two men had moved out of their seats and walked away without being asked so that we could sit. When the woman dumped the food onto the center of the table, I glanced around, waiting for someone to say something. This food display explained what the newspaper that had been spread over the center of the table had been for. Two more trays of tantalizing seafood mix were bought out and dumped on the table along with some saucers of lemon wedges and packages of lemon wet wipes.

When the seven remaining men, Israel, and his brother started digging in, I followed suit, opting for a piece of corn. The spicy-sweet flavor was delicious enough for me to try a few of the mussels.

At first, it appeared everyone was tossing their shells and cobs on the floor, but a glance down showed metal buckets placed around the table at our feet. I'd never eaten this way before, but this would certainly be a lunchtime to remember. The men were yelling around the table in three different conversations, all about different sports.

Micah spoke but kept his smiling observation on me and Israel like he sensed something that I wasn't aware of. The rest of the bar wasn't being discreet about studying me with him either, especially when he kept leaning over to make sure I was okay, handing me more corn and mussels, and draping his arm around the back of my seat possessively.

We sat for hours as I watched people mosey up to the table and join in for a few bites to eat, jump in and out of the multiple conversations going on, and eyeball Israel's new property—me. Oddly, I started to make sense of Israel's earlier words while watching the way the men, as dangerous as I sensed they were, regarded the patch-wearing women with respect, even when some of the women were allowing alcohol to make their decisions.

The group had questions about me, but I was starting to think that MC's rules didn't allow them to question Israel's decision where it regarded me. They didn't have to worry about me stealing their *Snake Eyes* away for long because Major would straighten things out, and I'd be out of their hair in no time.

Tired of hearing about carries, punts, and field goals, I cleaned my hands until they were lemony fresh and leaned over to Israel. He leaned down to meet me halfway as I put my lips to his ear. "I need to use the bathroom," I whispered. All of the spotlight attention I had been receiving had my bladder fisting and my pee knocking to get out.

Israel pointed to an opening that led into a dimly lit hall. "Right over there," he said. "I'll wait here for you." I was hesitant to step away, sensing that all eyes remained on me, although heads weren't pointed in my direction. I put my big girl panties on, took a deep breath, and stepped away.

Getting into and out of the bathroom was seamless. The men's bathroom was directly across the hall from the ladies, and the only thing that kept the doors from being perfectly aligned with one another was a painting of a big metal skeleton riding a motorcycle.

As soon as I stepped out of the bathroom, the sight of the man standing in front of that large painting outside the men's restroom stopped me in my tracks. A deep gasp rushed in as my hand gripped my chest. Like all the men in this compound, this one was tall, well built, and dressed in black from head to toe with the MC's cut.

Was his face scarred? I couldn't tell from the black baseball cap he wore that was pulled low enough that I only caught a tiny flash of his eyes. There was something about his presence that stilled me when I probably should have been running. It was like standing in the center of a bed of ants that were crawling all over my body, and waiting for him to give them permission to start biting me.

He took a step towards me, and I yanked back, bumping into the closed door I had just stepped out of. He appeared to be floating closer, and the loud music and noise that had followed me into the hall had faded into the background. What I assumed were scars were tattoos on his face at his temples, and there were some reaching up from his neck. He was a state of perpetual darkness, with not so much as a trace of emotion in him. He had the presence of a dead man.

"Have you ever seen the skin get peeled off a human skull?" His voice had goosebumps popping up on my skin. If I hadn't just used the bathroom, his question would have had piss running down my legs. "Do you know a woman still gets wet after she's dead?"

Help! Israel, please help! The loud voice screaming inside my head refused to pass across my lips. "I can show you if you'd like to see," the man said like we were having a casual conversation. I'd been around some scary people, but this one was straight from the lowest level of hell. He was no doubt the devil's BFF.

"I see you've met Severe." Israel's voice was that of an angel. I didn't care how it looked. I ran into him, gripping him around the waist like he was my man. He threw his arms around me with ease, tucking me into his chest.

"Have you been scaring Zyana, cousin?" he asked the living nightmare that I was glad I couldn't see anymore.

"She appeared to have a thirst for knowledge, and I'm always willing to share it," he said, his voice heavy and dark behind me. His light steps faded like that of a ghost as he walked away without saying another word.

"Is he crazy? Touched?" I asked Israel, glancing up.

"No. The opposite actually. He enjoys scaring people. It's his defense mechanism to keep everyone at a distance, but he's one of the most loyal people I know."

I didn't care what Israel said; his cousin was a damn psychopath. Talking about peeling skin from skulls and dead wet pussy. Major had prepared me for a lot. He'd shown me how to shoot, taught me self-defense, and a few other basic survival skills. But there was one thing he couldn't teach me, and that was how to live among a bunch of killers, murderers, and homicidal lunatics.

"You ready to go home?" Israel asked, glancing down. I still hadn't unwrapped myself from him.

"I'm not going to lie to you. Your people are scarier than an uprising in hell."

He released a low chuckle before he turned us back into the bar with me clinging to him despite the fact that I had been fighting to get away from him less than twenty-four hours ago. For now, my days of running from Israel Sylas were officially over.

CHAPTER SIX

Zyana

Once we stepped outside the bar, we returned to the motorcycle to pick up Israel's backpack that was stuffed with my clothes and personal items. We left the Harley parked in place and hiked along a trail leading past the bar until it appeared we were about to walk into the thick vegetation that hid the ground and formed a living set of shaggy curtains.

We trekked closer to a thick wooden bridge that was built up above the wetlands and cut through a congested patch of trees and vines. The beauty of the scenery was postcard-worthy with photo ops at every blink of the eye. We approached the sturdy bridge and hiked along its wooded path that branched off in different directions to what I believed were other member's homes.

We'd covered a good distance before reaching the end of the bridge that connected to Israel's low sloping porch. His house was built above the wetlands so that you could glance across the porch railing and peer down at the wet floor covered in beautiful flowering plants and greenery. Once we'd stepped fully onto the porch, I realized we were at the side of the house.

When we turned the bend and stepped around to the front, I stopped in my tracks. The house faced an opening that showcased a spectacular view of the body of water I'd spotted earlier. The setting sun's rays bounced off the waves, making the water appear to wink at me.

We were so far into the swamps that I had no idea where we were geographically. All I knew was that this was one of the most beautiful places I'd been to. It was in direct contrast to the reputation of the people who lived here.

"Wondering how a bunch of rednecks could afford all of this?"

"Yeah. I mean. This is a beautiful place. It's like you found a way to respect nature enough that you can co-exist. Aside from all of the big bikers, it feels like I'm at a retreat."

"My brothers and I inherited the land from our mother. She died of cancer when we were twelve. We decided to finally do something with the land after our father was killed."

"You said when *we* were twelve. And last night when you mentioned my brother helping your brother, you also said, when *we* were twenty-six. Does that make you and your brothers triplets?"

He grinned. "It looks like being the sister of a top-notch detective pays off because most people wouldn't have caught that. Many still have no idea that we were born only minutes apart because we have always embraced our individuality. They know us more for being a terror all our lives, three demons set free to unleash hell on earth. Believe it or not, I'm the tame one."

My unblinking stare caused him to grin harder. "You, the tame one—" I said, shaking my head and flashing him a dismissive smirk. "How old are you guys? Who's the youngest of you three?"

"Thirty-two and me," he replied. The notion of him being the youngest triplet caused me to crack a wide grin that mirrored his. Why were there long stare offs happening between us now? To break the unusual tension, I approached the thick wooden rails edge of the porch and took in the scene.

The water and trees co-existed in a way I had never seen in person. Their thick trunks were submerged as the fluttering water encircled it like a flowing skirt. The insect calls were like unscripted instrumentals being harmonized.

"Oh shit!" I shouted, jumping back from the rail when a snake swam by like it didn't have a care in the world. Israel stepped closer, taking in the slithering monster that had scared the shit out of me.

"It's a baby water moccasin. Sometimes they get into the house, so I'd advise you to stay close," he said, and he wasn't smiling.

"Please tell me you're kidding."

He didn't answer, only stepped away, unlocked and twisted the front door open, and waited until I walked in first.

Wow! Just as the first sight of the compound had taken me by surprise, the inside of Israel's house did as well. Rustic, bold, beautiful. The theme outside matched the inside as it was decorated with mostly natural and aged-wood furnishings.

Like his boat, this place was neat, clean, and well-kept. The high ceilings were hollowed to show off the dimensions of the cabin's structure. Everything was open, and the front wall was all windows that presented a splendid view of the water.

A quick once-over of the cabin's interior revealed that there was one bedroom. Not that I had been checking for it, but there wasn't a single sign of a woman, lending truth to his earlier comment that he'd never bought one home.

"You didn't eat much at lunch, and it's nearing dinner time. Are you hungry?" he asked.

The way my stomach had started grumbling, he'd probably heard it from across the room.

"I could eat," I replied.

"I can make a few things, but breakfast and spaghetti are all I do well."

He handed me the remote to the television.

"Either sounds good," I replied, taking the remote.

"Spaghetti, it is," he said before walking off.

I toed off the cheap slip-ons that we had picked up from the dollar store and tucked my legs under me and into the rust-colored soft-leather couch. Absently, I flipped through the channels while pretending not to eyeball Israel's every move in his kitchen.

If there was one thing I was certain about, it was that Israel was an outlaw, a savage, a deadly force I would hate to meet under different circumstances. Although he had the living off the grid part down, he was more domesticated than I would have given him credit for.

He used a colander to drain the spaghetti before setting the steaming, delicious-smelling meat sauce to a low simmer. When he turned in my direction, I fixed my eyes on the television, knowing damn well I wasn't watching the history channel. For some reason, his approach set my pulse to a quick thump, and he didn't stop until he was standing in front of me, way too close.

"Here. Major just text that he'd like to speak to you." I took the phone, hearing it ringing before I had it up to my ear.

"Zyana—"

"Major—" We called to each other as soon as the lines connected. Israel stepped away, heading towards the bedroom.

"Are you okay? In danger? Being careful?" I knew that my brother could handle himself, but it didn't stop me from worrying about him.

"I'm good. Making progress on getting this resolved. I need you to stay with Israel a little bit longer. He told me you guys were at Ground Zero. How are you? How's he been treating you?"

"I'm okay. It's all just a bit of culture shock. Israel is— He's. Okay," I stated, not knowing how to answer the question. He was one of the most dangerous men I knew, yet once I stopped fighting him, I could see that he was only trying to protect me. Now, I wondered if I had some weird dark attraction to the man.

"He told me how you two know each other," I told Major in a teasing tone.

"He did!" Major shouted into the phone, followed by a low muttering of curse words.

"I may be your kid sister, but I think I have proven that I *can* handle the darker subject matters," I told him. "With that being said, will you tell me what's really going on with this case?"

A long silence followed before he cleared his throat. "Although I know Israel put you on a secure line, I don't want to say much over the phone. However, I do know that the leak came from someone we both know. One of my informants may be able to get us a link that may lead us to the rat. Once we find him—"

Someone was speaking to him low in the background. "Look, I gotta go. Love you, sis."

"Be careful. Love you too," I said, my throat going tight with worry at his sudden departure.

After a long moment of staring at the phone in my hand, I used it to access the internet. Israel had let me use it to call work and my friends before we'd left his boat, and I'd also used it to check my emails.

A while later, and although I hadn't heard a sound, the sudden appearance of Israel's shadow looming over me made me jump. The man could sneak up on silence and make it speak.

"What are you doing?" he said, jerking his phone from my hand. He pressed the button to call up what had taken my attention enough for him to sneak up on me.

"Messy Mandy?" he asked, staring at what I had been reading. "The Lunchtime Dish." He kept reading. He'd caught me in the act of enjoying one of my guilty pleasures, soaking in all the gossip I could handle from one of my favorite social media pages.

"Let me guess — you thought I was calling out for help?"

He nodded but hadn't taken his eyes off the phone yet. He tapped the screen a couple of times, and I heard, *"It's me, Messy Mandy."* Mandy's words sounded in that uniquely quirky voice of hers, and I could picture her Avatar shaking her little head on the screen.

Israel listened and smiled while Mandy was dishing about the latest and greatest gossip. The more she talked, the wider his smile grew before his stare became fixed with a pensive glint on mine.

"I think I get why you like this. It's like SportsCenter for gossip." My eyes widened, surprised by his accurate assessment. He handed the phone back and walked away without any further words.

"Well, Messy Mandy, although he'll never admit it, it looks like you just got yourself another fan," I mumbled to myself as my eyes followed Israel retreating into the kitchen.

***

It felt like only minutes had passed since we'd sat on the couch together eating our spaghetti and watching old sitcoms. I startled awake, and like I'd done on the boat, I was using Israel's firm pec for a pillow, and my hand was sitting on his hard bulge.

I didn't move my hand right away. There was no use in lying to myself — I was attracted to the man. I had seen him naked, gawked at him showering, and sat on his dick while riding backward on his motorcycle. There weren't many secrets we had left, and I hadn't known the man a full twenty-four hours.

The deep rise and fall of his chest indicated that he was asleep. My attempt to feed myself the lie that he'd been the one staging my hand over his dick failed because I'd fallen asleep thinking about it. There was no doubt that the unconscious part of me had done what my conscious mind wasn't willing to.

Although consumed by the way his firm body pressed into mine, I eased up. Damn, he was sexy. He was someone I would never have given a second look to if I'd met him in passing because I would have been too busy profiling him like I'd done last night.

I wouldn't have considered that he was more than what he presented on his surface. I would have missed that, despite the way he looked, he had a caring nature, strong protective instincts, and those mesmerizing green eyes had the incredible ability to hold a lifetime in a single stare.

Instead of getting up like I had intended to, I laid my head back on his chest, carefully placed my hand back on his thick bulge, and allowed sleep to lull me back under.

CHAPTER SEVEN

Israel

A week later.

When Zyana was comfortable enough to stay home alone, I started leaving to help her brother. I had shown her around the compound enough that anyone with a pulse knew she was mine even if she didn't.

Conventional measures weren't getting the job done, so Major had requested my assistance in catching his man and disassociating Zyana's identity from the underground. The relentless pursuit seemed to tighten the unusual bond we had formed with each other.

Me, being what Major called a modern-day outlaw and him, the non-traditional lawman, weren't supposed to be friends, but here we were, hunting together. However, this was the second time in our decade-long history that we had banded together for a shared *personal* reason.

Wait a damn minute. Had I allowed my brain to admit that I was no longer doing this as a favor, but as a personal quest? What the hell did that mean? *Fuck it.* I knew exactly what it meant. I cared for Zyana more than I wanted to admit, and I damn sure wasn't telling her brother.

Major may have played the law-abiding citizen and by-the-book cop in front of the department, but I knew better. I'd borne witness to what had gone down during a few of his deep cover operations. The man would put a bullet in someone who deserved it faster than I could snap a finger, and like me, he knew how to make a body disappear as masterfully as a seasoned magician.

He and I had hunted common enemies on several occasions, men who sought to come after my MC for one reason or another, and men who'd committed heinous crimes that Major had to prove in the eyes of the criminal justice system.

There were times I did him the favor of killing them if he was unable to gather the proof needed to convict them. There were times he'd have an unexpected shoot out when he knew it was someone hiding from me that needed to be dealt with.

Usually, I didn't appreciate the difficulties we faced to solve the problem, but this time I was enjoying the company of my houseguest and welcomed the roadblocks, even if it meant flirting with a lingering danger. The idea of coming home to a beautiful woman every day was not something I'd pictured for myself, but there was something special about Zyana that made me add her to my priorities list.

She and I were from such different worlds that I couldn't imagine us cultivating a working relationship, but I'd be damned if I didn't spend time wondering *what if.* She couldn't cook for shit, but by the time I made it home every day, she'd have soaked in all of the Messy Mandy she could stand on my secure laptop, the house would be clean, and she'd have half-burned a dinner that I would eat like it was a gourmet meal.

I wanted to fuck her so badly that I ached all over, and my dick readied itself for a search and destroy mission whenever she was within my reach. She'd taken up the habit of falling asleep against me every night. Somehow, she managed to burrow herself in so tightly, that I was left with no choice but to wrap her up like the gift she'd turned out to be.

Now, while rolling through the compound's front gate, I regarded the guys with grunts and quick waves because I was in a hurry to see her. When I rounded the bend of my porch, I found her sitting in one of the lounge chairs with her gaze fixed on the view of the water. Usually, late June brought in extreme bouts of humidity and heat, but the temperature had been unseasonably pleasant.

Seeing her face light up at the sight of me put a funny twinge in my chest that had me rubbing at the area. The faint sound of music seeping from the house through the screened outer door deepened the smile she had put on my face.

Rock or heavy metal was what I usually played during my waking hours. Hearing her sing along to some of the tunes hinted at her open-mindedness and had me wondering if she was as impartial about who she dated and slept with. She was attracted to me, I had no doubt about that, but attraction didn't always translate into a willingness to embrace the next level.

"You're not afraid of the snakes and insects anymore?" I asked, remembering how she'd been glued to my side each time we went outside, batting at the insects and searching for snakes.

Her easy smile made her eyes sparkle. "It took me a minute to understand that the animals are relaxing in their peaceful settings as much as I am. It's like we're respecting each other's space now."

The idea of her calling my place peaceful had me downplaying a deep grin while I was taking the seat next to her.

"Did you burn us some dinner today?" I asked, fighting, but failing, to keep in a laugh.

She smacked my arm, leaving a little peppery sting that I liked. "I made chicken alfredo, and you will be happy to know that it's not burned."

I nodded, knowing that if it wasn't burned, the noodles would be over or undercooked, or the chicken may be frozen on the inside. She had no concept of the right time to combine the dishes she made, and me attempting to show her made it worse. It had taken me a while to learn the mechanics of cooking, so I figured time was her only hope.

The notion that Major and I were another step closer to resolving the case added to the heavy ache that roared to life at the idea of Zyana leaving. Each time she asked about the progress of our hunt, I'd skirt the subject.

"Can I ask you something, and you give me an honest answer?" she asked, staring under those thick lashes at me with one brow lifted.

My stare met hers, burrowing in deep enough to catch that exact moment it stirred her discomfort. "I haven't lied to you yet."

She dropped her eyes, and I didn't miss the small smile that touched her lips before she lifted them to recapture my waiting gaze.

"I assumed a lot of stuff about you, judging a book by its cover and all. Now that you've brought me to this place, I don't know what to think. The gunfire I hear sometimes—" she said, pointing in the direction of our gun range that I had taken her to see the second day she was here.

"—The way the word 'outlaw' gets tossed around about your MC. The way everyone around here has that look in their eyes like they aren't afraid to march straight into hell and confront the devil. Instead of assuming about you and your MC, I figured I'd check before speculating this time. What do you guys do for a living?"

She sat her hope-filled gaze on mine, unaware that I didn't have shit to hide from her. I wasn't her brother, and I wasn't going to place her in a bubble of protection that could get popped by anyone or anything.

"We sell protection, the kind you can't walk into a store and buy or purchase online."

"Guns?" she asked.

My head shook in the negative. "The authorities suspect that we sell guns or drugs and we let them think it, knowing they will never prove it. Their assumptions provide the perfect cover for what we really sell."

"What do you sell?" she asked, almost breathless with curiosity.

"We sell protection, like what I'm doing with you, but for much more dangerous and high-profile people. However, our main product involves selling a more *permanent* solution to people who may find themselves stuck in deadly situations. We track down their problems and provide a solution."

She allowed my words to soak in, her eyes flicking left to right before they widened. She leaned closer and whispered, "You guys are hitmen?"

"Our MC isn't named Hell *Reapers* because it has a nice ring to it. When someone puts in an order for a reaping, a soul is claimed and collected," I told her, holding her wide, unblinking gaze.

Grinning at the awed expression she flashed, I stood and prepared to enter the house. *If she only knew how many people I've killed for her brother,* I thought, shaking my head.

CHAPTER EIGHT

Israel

Later, we assumed our usual positions on the couch. It always started with us sitting apart before she would ease closer and let her head fall against my shoulder. I would play along and turn so that her body would be snuggled into mine.

Tonight, I couldn't wait through the game we played and hauled her smoothly into my lap, dragging until she was straddling my legs. She sat, stunned, her wide gaze aimed at mine until I leaned in for a kiss that she didn't turn down.

The impact of our lips touching sent heat racing through my veins before I slid a hand behind her neck and the other over her ass. I pressed my lips harder against her mouth, deepening the kiss before my tongue slid between her plump lips. The fresh flavor of her plush mouth, so warm and wet, was like a touch of dark magic penetrating my body. The smooth sweeps of her lips gliding so firmly against mine had me gripping her tight enough to cause pain.

I adjusted her against me, making my stiff erection fit into the V that parted her thighs. The action made her lose her breath as her quick pants breezed against my lips, the sound flirting with my earlobes and making love to my mind.

"I'm tired of you teasing my dick and not doing anything about it. Touch it," I commanded, shoving her hand down between us. I busied one hand with one of her lush ass cheeks and kept the other behind her neck to keep her in place to prolong our heated kiss.

Her stroke was light along the rigid edges of my shaft, her hand running up and down the length before she began to squeeze and stroke harder and faster. Thankfully, I had showered and put on sweatpants.

"Fuck this," I growled. "Take these fucking clothes off," I barked, not caring that I sounded like a demanding asshole because she was into this as much as me. She sent a few lingering flicks across my lips with her exploring tongue and pressed her lips into mine with a final smack before she backed off. She stood in front of me, taking her sweet time removing her clothes, giving me a show.

She peeled my t-shirt she wore up her body, exposing a silky blue bra before she tossed the shirt at me, landing it on my head. I took a quick sniff before tossing the shirt around my neck like a towel. She slid her shorts down her legs, and the fluidity of her body movements captured my hungry gaze that traced every tempting curve. Shapely brown hips and thighs moved seductively and kicked up my urge to spread them and feast on her.

The shape her pussy print made in those tiny blue panties had my full attention. Since the first night we'd met, I wanted nothing more than to bury my face in her pussy before I explored the area extensively with my dick.

"Wait. Let me help you with that," I told her, standing. My throat had gone dry because the sight of her had made me thirstier than a motherfucker. She had my whole body jittery and overflowing with a palpable energy that I needed to expend. I'd never been like this for a woman, burning so hot, I could be the replacement for hellfire.

Her hand slid over my hot skin when I stepped closer and didn't stop until she was caressing my straining erection. I reached around and unsnapped her bra with a quick twist of my fingers.

"Have you ever had anything that big?" I asked as her hand continued to pet it like the fucking animal it was becoming.

She shook her head. "No. I can't say that I have."

"Think you can handle it?"

She shrugged, but the sneaky grin on her face was speaking her thoughts. "I don't know. My mind is telling me to be cautious, but my neglected pussy is saying, "You got this, bitch.""

That's my fucking girl. She was speaking bold words while holding what was still growing and uncurling in my pants. I loved that she was letting me see that feisty side of her personality I liked so much.

The bra went sliding across the floor after I tossed it aside, and a second later, one of her dark tips grazed my tongue. I placed a kiss on each, making them pucker even tighter. My hand ran possessively down her body, leaving a trail of goosebumps on her warm silky skin. The sight fed into my ravenous state of mind, fueling a hunger I'd never experienced.

My hands worked their way down until my fingers were hooked on either side of the thin waistband of her panties. Ripping them would be too quick and easy. I wanted to enjoy the sight of them sliding along her skin and dragging over those delicious curves.

The way she swayed and quaked when I slid her panties over her ass and watched the wet center separate from her pussy lips had me swallowing my impulsive need to fuck her like a caged beast. The sight of those thin wet panties slipping down her legs had my dick jumping and my mind on sensory overload. I wanted her so badly that my tongue was lapping at my lips like I could already taste her arousal just from the scent alone.

Once I had the panties off, she watched me lift them to my nose and all but inhale them. There was no doubt in my mind that I had fibers from her panties floating around in my lungs.

Without warning, I shoved until I backed her into the wall from my bent position and with my hungry tongue, licked up the soft, warm skin of her leg like a starved dog. The action set off a visible shiver in her body as I used the backs of my hands against her soft inner thighs to spread her legs open further.

I bit deep into the inside of her left thigh, the nip making her push out a loud moan. The bite also made her pussy slicker, and a rush of liquid heat surfaced like the sticky-sweet juices squeezed from fresh fruit.

When I guided my tongue closer to the heat source, I gripped her above the backs of her knees before lifting and positioning myself between them so that only her back was pressed against the wall. A deep groan bubbled up my throat when my starved tongue licked across her slick lower lips.

"You're so fucking wet. I love the way your sweet juices are pouring over my tongue," I whispered against her as I leaned forward to lick at the essence flowing down her inner thigh. I realigned my face with her pussy before leaning into her flowing heat and allowing it to consume my lips and my mouth. A low possessive growl crawled from my chest before I inhaled a deep breath that allowed me to take in her heady scent.

I backed away to look at the area that had my face wet, unable to help running my fingers between her lips. Back and forth and back again, I slid my fingers over her pussy, toying with her pulsing clit with my thumb. Her nails dug deeper into my shoulders as she shuddered, her head thrown back against the wall and rocking from side to side like I was delivering the gospel that was soaking into her spirit.

"Fuck, I gotta have another taste. I want you all over my fucking tongue and all down my throat," I groaned out my words as my quick breaths bounced off her pussy and made her gasp. The sexy, anxious sounds she made rushed out in quick pants as she teetered against the wall like her whole body had gone weak.

I drew closer to secure her in place, my tongue ready, and my mind anticipating the moment her hot sex landed over my taste buds again. A fresh hot shot bloomed over my tongue, and there was no stopping the ravenous urge I had to eat her alive. She was like a sweet, hot fruity punch that I was instantly addicted to.

"Fuck, your pussy's good," I couldn't help saying. "Mmm." The flavor had me moaning in pleasure, the sound traveling along my skin and echoing through my dick. For the first time in my life, taste was a tool that sharpened my arousal. The shit had me iron hard.

I raked my tongue across her lower lips before slipping it between them and finally curving it up and shoving it deep into her where the heat level scorched my taste buds. Once I had my tongue inside, I waved it, lapping at the quivering flesh that pressed against my tongue while my top lip kissed her clit.

"Shit. That's it!" she screamed as she managed to grip my hair, raking her nails through my scalp.

She shoved the outer layers of her pussy against my chin and nose, taking advantage of more than my mouth. "Israel! Fuck! Oh!" She heaved out. "I need. I want. I'm—"

She came hard, and I felt it all. The internal jerks pushing at my tongue, her sweet nectar flowing into my mouth, and her thighs quaking and knocking against the sides of my head as she fell apart. It was the most beautiful thing I'd ever seen and hotter than flames stolen from hell.

She looked so fucking sexy, all laid back against the wall and spread open for me. Her parted mouth, tightly-shut eyes, and tensed and twitching muscles caused a satisfied smile to surface on my lips. The way her chocolate-tipped nipples tightened and her ample globes bobbed with the harsh push and pull of her breaths added fuel to my amped-up passion.

Not giving her time to recover, I gripped one of her arms and shook it to get her to retract her nails from my shoulder so that I could ease her feet down to the floor. With a tight grip on her upper arm, I led her to the couch, steadying her swaying body.

My finger was aimed at the spot I wanted her in, on the couch. "On your knees. Hold on to the couch back. Tightly. You're going to need it," I warned her. I walked around to the back of the couch to face her in the kneeling position she was in, preparing to give her a show by stripping my shirt off and tossing it at her.

It landed on her head and right shoulder, making her smile, but she tilted to the side and let it fall beside her. Her tongue slid hungrily across her lips, leaving them wet at the sight of me about to shove my pants down.

I wasted little time, gripping the waistband of my sweats and stripping them down my legs. My dick was so hard and heavy, it popped out and slapped against my stomach before returning to a standing position.

"*Shit,*" she mouthed silently, her eyes glued to my stiff dick like she'd never seen one before. I kicked the pants off my feet before strolling up to her with my dick pointed right at her mouth. I didn't have to say shit, as she let her lips fall apart and opened her mouth wide.

The leaking tip kissed her top lip before I pushed it inside her mouth and felt her hot tongue massaging the underside of my shaft. "Look up, baby," I requested, wanting to see those big and pretty brown eyes while I fucked her mouth. She did, and I didn't have to give her any more instructions as she worked, slipping a hand over my shaft and working my fucking balls like they were clay in her hands.

She slid me in and out of her mouth, slowly at first, but picking up the pace and tightening the sucking action that had me losing my fucking mind. The harder she sucked, the deeper she took me until I was knocking at the back of her throat that responded by caressing the head. The glorious pressure of the tight squeeze had me fighting the delicious ache that was traveling up my dick and pulsing through me like high wattage electricity.

"That's it, baby. Take me deeper. Suck…that…dick." I choked out each word, fighting to keep my eyes from rolling in my head. I needed to see the stunning sight of her sucking me off and glancing up with all that lust in her eyes.

"Fuck!" The view made the pleasure flare. She had my glutes clenched, my thigh muscles pumping, and my abs pulled tight enough to snap. I was sure my curled toes had scratched a big-ass hole in the hardwood floor.

"Aww fuck!" I yelled out when the tip dipped down her throat. My damn head and neck veins were straining as tightly as my muscles, and my skin was burning so hot that I knew it was sunset red.

No longer able to control my actions, I gripped the back of her head and thrust in and dragged out, fucking her mouth to get back to sliding down her throat with each stroke. She was right there with me, gagging, sucking, and moaning all at the same time. The warm wetness of her mouth coated my dick. The sensation of the suction, mixed with the depth of her throat action, sparked a powerful tingle that reached my toes.

One final push and lightning strikes hit me and crackled down my back with such force that I lifted on the balls of my feet. I erupted down her throat, the tight space spasming around my jerking dick as she managed to move her mouth around the shaft.

"Fuck, Z. Fuuuuuk!" I roared at the top of my lungs as my grip on her hair tightened — most of the soft strands I'd worked loose from the ponytail. Her mouth and slick, waving tongue extended my orgasm, and the flow of cum shot out again, and again and a fucking 'gain.

I gripped the back of the couch so hard with my free hand that I ripped a hole in the soft leather. Her light sucks were making me shudder with each pull. I found the strength to pull out of her mouth, but she had me so turned on, I remained hard and hungry for that good-tasting pussy of hers.

The way Zyana had mouth-fucked me had been better than any of the community pussy I'd had, so I couldn't imagine the magic she held between her sexy legs.

CHAPTER NINE

Zyana

The name 'Snake Eyes' was starting to make sense. There was a fucking wild animal in Israel's pants, and if you stared directly in those intensely predatory eyes of his, you were going to become his victim.

He'd shot cum down my throat so hard, and for so long, I wasn't going to need to eat meat for a week. And dammit if it wasn't sweet like he'd eaten a perfectly-balanced fruit diet. I was still licking the inside of my mouth for the remnants of his taste when he sat those mesmerizing eyes on mine.

"Don't move," he ordered as he walked around the couch, his eyes stalking me, and mine aimed at his stiff, bobbing dick. With that thing, he was about to fuck some shit up, and I was about to let him.

He was behind me now, so quiet that it kicked up the tension in my body, and all I could do was dig my fingers deeper into the top of the couch to ready myself.

"Bend over, and lift that beautiful ass up high. We are going to get this pussy good and open so I can see my dick wreaking havoc on those pretty pink walls."

I did as I was told, although my heart danced in my chest, racing with a mixture of biting fear and intense excitement. Him ripping a condom open sounded and reminded me that I was so far gone that I hadn't even asked about protection. He didn't waste any time getting at me. The first hot contact made me jump.

"Relax. It's my fingers," he informed. "If it was my dick, trust me, you'd know it." He continued rubbing my pussy, dipping his fingers in and out until I was meowing like a kitten and wet enough to wash a load of clothes.

He placed his hands around my waist and yanked me back before sending a solid slap against my ass cheek, making it bounce. The spike of pain was a sweet one that had me licking my lips as my pussy pulsed and clenched. Another hard smack landed against the other cheek, the sting staying where it had landed before it dissolved over my flesh and sent a lusty hunger racing through me.

I was getting wetter from his delicious smacks, feeling my juices trickle down my inner thighs. *What the hell?* I'd been slapped on the ass before but had never reacted like this. He gave me two more smacks that sounded off, the fleshy licks adding to the mix of the sexual chemistry threatening to blow the roof off the cabin.

This time, when his hard heat touched me, I didn't jump because I was soaked and ready. The head licked at my lips, hungry, hot, and hard as steel. When he gave a push, splitting my pussy lips, I tightened my grip on the couch back. Eager to know how deep he would go and how it would feel to be opened by him, I deepened the arch in my back.

Another shove and he didn't stop as the thick length stretched my walls, spreading me wide open. The thrust went on for a lifetime and felt good enough to make me gasp with deep breaths of pleasure. A spark of pain was sprinkled in with the pressing desire, but the fulfilling tingles made my whole body quake with lust. I had no idea if he was all the way in, but he stopped and allowed me to adjust and didn't move again until I stopped shaking.

He eased back and shoved in farther this time, causing the hard, pressing heat to reach in so deeply, that I knew he hadn't had it all inside me that first time. He kept thrusting, going deeper each time and pumping harder until he filled me up to the point where I was sure I would spontaneously combust. I don't know what the hell his dick was telling my pussy, but with each stroke, the pleasure licked away the aches of my deepest desires.

"Oh shit! Oh fuck, fuck, fuck!" I yelled, loving the way he gripped my hips and waist and worked me up and down his dick, and up and back down to the point where he was the one controlling my breathing.

A glance back showed him arching into me with each rhythmic downstroke, every muscle tensed, teeth buried in this bottom lip. His heavy gaze met mine on a vicious downward movement and caused more lust to bloom in my core for him. Each long stroke would reach in and lick the back of my tunnel before punching at it and sparking a sensation that sent shockwaves up and down my straining walls and sensitive nerve endings.

"Oh shit! The dick. Fuck, you're fucking me right!" I was saying a mix of all kinds of crazy. Moaning, cursing, and yelling out to express my satisfaction. The impacting thrust had the couch moving as it grunted with each powerful stroke like it was a part of our episode.

Without interrupting his rhythm, he sent a loud smack across my ass that made my pussy clamp down on him. I wanted to look back and see his face, but I was under his full control, and if I didn't hold on, I may have ended up being fucked through the couch back.

His commanding thrusts had my chest slamming into the back of the sofa while I fought to keep a hold of it. The loud smacking sound of his dick and my pussy connecting was in tune with my screams. Pussy pulsing and dick slamming into the hilt, we were churning out the best fucking I had experienced in my life.

"Oh. Oh, Lord! I'm about to come!" I yelled, spitting words out like a robot, so loud I was sure the sound waves had busted the front door clean off the hinges. My body was ripped apart, my molecules sent in a hundred different directions, all of them infused with a powerful pleasure that wrecked me down to my curled toes.

His loud roar sounded, the vibrations from his thundering voice were like feather strokes to my quivering body. I was a fucking mess, shaking and twitching from the aftermath and somehow still finding a way to get off on him getting off, as the jerking of his dick and the hot flow of his cum into the condom had me moaning and continuing to pulse around him.

We froze where we were, my face on the top of the couch back, my fingers dug deep into the leather, and him gripping my hips as his hardness continued to jump inside me.

We didn't move again until our souls returned because I was sure we had scared them away from our bodies.

Israel eased his length out of me and fell into a sitting position on the couch. I couldn't move, so I stayed in position with my wet ass and pussy jacked up in the air. He was forced to grasp my waist and drag me into his lap to reanimate my body movements.

Sitting across his lap, he tucked me into his chest so that I was able to place my arms around his neck. "That was amazing," I whispered into his ear, my breaths still in a rush to get in and out of me. His smile lifted against my cheek before he eased back to stare in my face.

"*You* are amazing." He grinned. "You have the best pussy I've ever had," he added without hesitation. His compliment sent me back to the cloud he'd just had me floating on. I eased my heavy head into the nook of his neck, relaxing against him and allowing my breathing to return to a normal pace.

"Zyana, I have to admit, I thought you would be all good-girl, shy and meek, but you are hotter than a mother-fucker. Sexy as sin. You may not be a Reaper in the same way that I am, but you are definitely a Carolina Reaper."

Is that another compliment?" I asked him.

"Fuck, yes. Do you know what a Carolina Reaper is?"

I shook my head.

"It's one of the hottest peppers on the planet."

My brows lifted. Did he truly believe I was hot on that kind of level? Like he'd heard the question on my mind, he nodded.

"You get into me like pepper, and the searing heat seems to energize me. The fiery passion you give off when

I'm fucking you — I've never experienced anything like that before. You're like a blazing spice, an all-consuming flame. The kind of fire I want to get burned by," he said, grinning.

"I could say the same about you," I stated, his compliment making my cheeks burn as I grinned from ear to ear. I lowered my voice to a whisper. "I can still feel your dick scraping against the walls of my pussy and stretching me open. I still taste your sweet cum in my mouth. I still feel the head licking my back wall."

His tongue slipped over his sexy lips before he glanced down at my pussy, my words seeming to reignite his fire. His smile couldn't get any wider after those statements. Instead of causing more damage to my beat-up pussy, we sat there just breathing while my mind drifted in the aftermath of the best sex of my life.

A thought flared to life in my mind. "So, you named your MC after a pepper?"

He shook his head. "No. Our father started this club, and the official name is Hell Reapers. However, we're locally known as the Carolina Reapers for him and my mother, who was every bit an outlaw as him. Her first name was Carolina, and his road name was Reaper. He was the original Reaper, one of the best in the business with over two-hundred souls claimed."

Although shocked by what he was telling me, it also pleased me that he was so open and willing to share his history and personal life. All of a sudden, the need to kiss him rose in me like a storm, despite all the dick and pussy action we'd just had. My lips pressed delicately against his, tasting him slowly before pressing harder. We kept that tender vibe like we were exploring the other side of the spicy heat between us.

When I eased back and glanced up at him, the tight pull of the connection I believed had always been between us tugged on my mental focus, and my body followed. My thoughts sparked with an electric charge that had my gaze glued to his. My highjacked mind was useless at beating back the pulsing energy transferred between us that made me shiver and him shake.

The flash of knowing in his gaze added to the connection already radiating through me and landed on my damn pounding heart. Lord, talk some sense into me right now because as sure as my heart was picking up speed, I saw in him a reflection of what was coursing through me. Care and concern, and dammit, there was that other thing that I sure as fuck wasn't saying. I didn't even want to think it.

He and I leaned in for another kiss, not ready to even touch the other side of lust. The kiss deepened, and when tongue got involved, the heat rode the wave straight down to my throbbing clit before a hard stirring from him nudged my hip.

"Hope you're ready for round two," he stated. "I'm about to give that pussy a real workout, not some half-assed fuck. Pussy that good deserves better than the weak as shit you've been getting." His assessment was spot on, but how could he possibly know that I'd never been fucked right?

When he turned me so that I was straddling his strong thighs, I was flowing before the tip even licked at my wet lips. This time, when he slipped on a condom and pushed into me, I assumed I'd be more prepared, but found that at this angle, I had to adjust to his size, the same as when he'd had my ass in the air. But dear Lord in heaven, once I was fully seated on him, and he began moving along with my dancing hips, the sparks caught, and I let the fire burn me down to my rattling bones. He started snatching my ass down so hard on his dick, I lost my breath, not caring that I was damn-near suffocating.

Hell, no, we weren't done. He got me again on the floor and buried himself so far up my pussy, it left the sweet after-taste of our sex on my tongue, causing me to lose my damn mind in the process.

I'd heard the saying about a man marking what was his, and damn if Israel wasn't marking my ass so good, that I was biting into his neck as my naked ass squeaked against the hardwood floor.

The solid pressure of the wood under me made each of his thrusts punch hard and deep. So damn deep that I feared he'd drill me through the floor. One leg was over a muscled shoulder, and with each powerful thrust, it sent my foot hitting the seat of the couch cushion. The other leg was just flapping in the wind as I'd lost muscle control and had no choice but to take the brutal pounding he delivered.

I needed to let him know that my neck was wedged against the bottom of the couch, but he hit a spot that hurt so damn good, I had a full body spasm. "Fuck. Yes," I managed to squeeze out. Who the hell cared about a broken neck? The man was fucking me like he could heal all wounds. However, when the orgasm he gifted me powered through me like an enchantingly violent storm, I was afraid for my life.

CHAPTER TEN

Zyana

Five days and a lot of fucking the shit out of each other later, and I was sure that my ass had landed in a hotbed of trouble with Israel 'Snake Eyes' Sylas.

One, I was hooked on *the* dick. The man didn't have generic dick. His was a name brand. He had the dick of all dicks. The king of the dick jungle. King Ding-a-ling. Two, I cared about him now and stressed about him going out there to danger like I worried about my brother.

Did I mention he had put me under dick-nosis? He was the first Caucasian man I'd been with, and he'd gone and gotten me addicted to his dick. Was I weak? Was I getting over the sexual poverty I had been suffering before meeting him? Mental overload wasn't off the table either. Maybe he was the anchor in the shit storm that had spilled all over my life.

Now, I was sitting here, with my fucking leg about to shake clean off the bone because my nerves were stirred up so badly. Israel had informed me that they were close to catching the one who had blown my brother's cover and given me up to the bad guys. Being so close to catching their man meant they were exposed to more danger.

Israel had come home the last three days covered in bruises and cuts. I was no medical expert, but I believed the purple and black bruises on his back were what happened after you were shot with a bulletproof vest on. He pretended like it was nothing so I wouldn't worry, but his nonchalance about the danger poured fuel on my blazing nerves.

The call I'd received from my brother no less than twenty minutes ago had me pacing a hole in the hardwood floor. There had been shouting in the background on the other end of the line and what had sounded like muffled gunfire. When Major had yelled, "Let me call you back!" before the line went dead, my damn heart was up and running.

My ragged nerves had me sitting, standing, and spinning in circles before I sat and restarted the process. The phone pinged in my hand, and I didn't even give it a chance to complete the ring before I clicked it on.

"Hello! Major. Israel!" I yelled into the phone. "It's me," Major answered. The sound of his voice eased a little of my tension. "Are you okay? Is Israel all right?" I asked before he could get a word out.

"Why are you worried about that fool?" he asked. I believe he was going for playful, to ease the shaking tension in my tone, but it didn't work. "Is he all right, Major?" I yelled, my irritation had chewed through my last shred of patience.

"We're on our way there. He was shot and wouldn't let us take him to the hospital. The medical team they have on the compound should be at his house in a few minutes. Let them in so that they can be ready when we arrive."

"How bad is it? Is he okay?" A long pause had me on the verge of choking on the breath I was holding. "Is he all right?" I asked, my voice cracking so badly, I wasn't sure he understood the question.

"He took a slug in his right side. The bullet's still in him, and he's lost a lot of blood." The silence screamed during the long pause that followed.

"Zyana," Israel called into the phone, likely snatching the phone from Major.

"Are you okay?" I asked him while running to the door when footsteps sounded on the porch. Instead of one medic appearing at the door, a three-person trauma team had shown up. An older graying man, dressed in their signature black on black clothes with their MC's cut, a younger woman that I would have pegged for a gothic queen, and a male about my age with glasses, who resembled the older man enough that he must have been his son.

"I'm fine," Israel said. Those were the words I wanted to here. "I just need to get this bullet taken out." His voice was too weak. He didn't sound like the strong, rough-talking man I was sure I had fallen in love with, in less than two weeks.

"You don't sound okay. Don't you go trying to kick-the-bucket on me."

"I won't," he choked out before he started coughing, and the hacking sound sent chills racing through me.

"We'll be there in about ten minutes," Major said in rushed words. The idea that Israel could no longer speak said all I needed to know. He was hurt badly.

The medical team had wheeled in a big, folded table and three suitcases large enough to carry bodies. When they began rearranging furniture and setting up their makeshift in-house medical center, I stood, stunned for a minute.

The table was unfolded into a makeshift hospital bed, and the large suitcases contained every type of medical instrument and machine that the group was putting together and plugging in. They even had a small cooler with bags of o-positive blood on ice.

All I was good for was pacing and praying, hoping and wishing until heavy footsteps sounded. I ran through the front door, along with the medical crew. The sight of Israel being carried between Major and his crazy cousin, Severe, had chills rippling through me so fiercely, my feet had cemented to the spot I was standing in, as I stared with my mouth wide open.

Israel's gaze barely lifted to mine, his head moving listlessly on his shoulders as he forced a weak smile. The young medical girl politely moved my stiff body to the side to allow them to get him into the house and onto the table. I limped back into the house, my legs refusing to work properly as my eyes were glued to Israel's lifeless limbs swinging limply as they moved him.

The medical team swarmed him once he was stretched out on the table, shouting instructions at each other, cutting him out of clothes, checking his vitals, and thoroughly checking his body.

It took Major walking up to me and tucking me into a hug to wake me from the trance I was in. I slung my arms around my brother's torso, but I couldn't pull my gaze away from Israel. I didn't know where Severe had gone, but he was no longer in the room.

"Are you hurt?" I asked Major, mindful enough to pat at his chest and torso.

"I'm fine, sis," he replied, glancing down at me with a sad glint in his gaze that he tried to but couldn't hide. He cared about Israel too, more than he would ever admit to me. But, he didn't have to admit it because the tortured expression on his face spoke for him.

"Who did this?" I asked Major. "Who was the asshole that blew your cover and exposed me?"

"Your ex, Kevin. The motherfucker failed at pimping you out to Big Stan of the West End Crew, so he slithered his ass up to Kinx, the head of the Murda Mafia. He must have spotted me somewhere and snitched."

"Is he—?"

"Yes," Major answered, knowing the question on my mind. I had stopped Major from killing Kevin the first time he'd done me wrong, but this time Major hadn't asked permission. I didn't know if it was good or bad that I didn't feel anything about his death.

"So, how did you get Kinx to forget I existed and to stop trying to kill you for infiltrating his operation? He's not someone that reasons with people."

The arrogant smirk on my brother's face told me all I needed to know. Major had charmed his way into the heart of a monster, and as sure as my name was Zyana, I knew he and Israel had done it together with a high body count.

"Let's just say everyone can be reasoned with," he said before letting a heavy silence fall between us.

Time dragged on like a second hand while I stood in my brother's arms watching the team work their asses off, shoving needles here and there, hooking up machines to various parts of Israel's body, and cleaning the sight of where the bullet had entered his side. They had put him to sleep, and seeing him that way sank me deeper into despair.

A machine produced a grainy image that showed them where the bullet was located. The trajectory indicated that the hot lead had traveled halfway through his body before an internal organ had stopped it.

When they started slicing his side open, I closed my eyes, and it took deep, desperate breaths to keep from throwing up. Major dragged me to the couch and tucked me into his side as the sound of the beeping machines and packages of whatever medical supplies they were using were ripped open.

My head lay planted against Major's arm while I prayed, putting my eyes back on Israel's unmoving body. "Z," Major said, receiving my low grunt as a reply. "Is there something you need to tell me about you and Israel?" he asked in an authoritative tone. He still hadn't accepted that the tone had no effect on me. "If I didn't know any better, I'd think you were acting like a stressed girlfriend."

"I have nothing to tell you, just like you had nothing to tell me for the ten years you'd known him," I stated, with so much attitude punctuating my words, Major bent so his face was in front of mine to obstruct my view of Israel.

"Are you two a couple?" he questioned.

Straightening myself, I stared straight into his eyes. "What if we are?" I replied with a question of my own. No one I dated was good enough in my brother's eyes. A few of the assholes he'd been right about, but still.

His body tensed, and his lips drew into a tight knot. "I'm killing him when he wakes up."

"So, let me get this straight. He's good enough to be your friend, but not good enough to date me?"

"Nope," he said, and gave me the eye like I should have known better. Once he was done staring me down, he stared back and forth between me and Israel like he couldn't make the connection.

"I'm killing him," Major decided before he tugged me back into his embrace.

I returned the caress, but mouthed, "No. You're not." Against his thick shoulder. "You said you wanted me to find someone who makes me happy. He does. I know what kind of world he's from, and have no damn idea how we are going to make this work, but seeing him like that, and knowing that he was helping you and fighting to keep me safe, is all the motivation I need to at least try."

Major stared like he didn't know me, his brows pinched tight, his eyes squinted into slits. "I'm still killing him. I picked him to protect you because I knew he was the best, but I was also sure you weren't his type, and he wasn't yours either."

"So, let me get this straight, again. You picked who would protect me based on what you thought my type was? You're as crazy as him," I pointed out.

"I don't want you associated with anyone I know, sis. I might work within the scope of the law, but a lot of my friends live outside it, and I don't want you dragged into more shit because of me."

I leaned up and placed a quick peck on his cheek. "You are a great big brother. The best. But, you can't protect me from everything. Besides, I've seen Israel in action, and I don't think I have too much to worry about where it concerns my safety."

Major didn't render a reply, but the mean-mugging look he was throwing Israel's way was his final word.

CHAPTER ELEVEN

Israel

The struggle to peel my eyes apart shouldn't have been this damn difficult. My consciousness was returning in a haze. *Shot. Side. Returned fire.* I had taken out three before an explosion of pain tried to overcome me, but thoughts of Zyana had kept me going. She was so beautiful. So feisty. Sweet. Sexy. Spicy. And she was mine.

"That's it, open those beautiful green eyes." The voice of an angel was coaxing me to open, and I damn sure was going to listen. *Zyana.* She was my heaven on earth, and I would fight the devil and all his disciples to get back to her.

My hand tightened around hers before the soft press of her lips brushed my forehead. "That's it. Let me see you," she whispered. I sprang the locks holding my lids together, and there she was. It felt like a fucking team of bears had mauled my side and snatched all the skin and tissue clean from my bones, but the sight of her eased my biting pain. I lay there with a silly smile while she sprinkled kisses all over my face.

When she eased back, a dark cloud loomed behind her. My vision focused, and the tall figure filled my view. *Major.* His arms were folded over his big broad chest, and his eyes were two brown fireballs in his head.

"Welcome back, motherfucker," he spit out, his face so serious, I expected to see him snatch his pistol and aim it at me. Zyana had undoubtedly told him about us.

She reached back blindly and smacked him across the leg. "Stop it. You were the one who called him into this mess, so stop being a dick," she barked back at her brother with a crooked smile.

He and I locked eyes for a long moment before he let a tiny sliver of a smile skate across his lips. He pointed and shook a stiff finger at me. "You son of a bitch. You hurt my sister, and I'm taking your dead, stinking body to the secret garden."

I gave a nod, acknowledging that I understood. The secret garden was in these swamps, a graveyard for all the worthless fucks we'd killed and had yet to kill.

Zyana playfully tapped her brother's arm at his comment, clueless, that friend or not, if I did anything to hurt her, Major would find a way to kill my ass, even if it meant him coming with me.

Casting aside death and mayhem at my friend's hands, I concentrated on the woman who'd sparked a fire in my otherwise dull life. She cast a long stare at my bandaged side before she leaned down to my ear.

"How long before we could get some *alone* time again?" I turned my face into her hair, "As soon as we can get the medical team back in here so that they can surgically remove your brother's deadly stare from my face."

We grinned, staring into each other's eyes, the depth of our attraction casting all other matters away. Did she know that I would kill anyone that even thought about coming between us? My smile deepened when the answer popped into my head. I wholeheartedly believed Zyana had a good idea of what it meant to be loved by a Reaper.

End of Carolina Reaper

**Please stay tuned for an excerpt from
Author Siera London**

Author Siera London – Excerpt

Red Velvet
Lunchtime Chronicles Book 20
By Siera London w/a S. London
Coming November 4, 2020

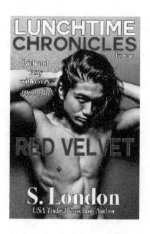

Mī Fantajī -Siah

My back hits the palatial windows overlooking the Sicilian countryside, and for a second, I'm an excited tourist visualizing the jaw-dropping street view of Knox's hands gripping my ass. Despite the sunny spring morning, the glass feels cool and dry against my skin. I expect the chill to spread through my limbs, but his body cocoons me in warmth. Like the air trapped in my lungs, he holds my orgasm hostage, stretching the minutes to mind-bending hours. Thanks to Knox, my vaginal vacation is officially women's history. I knew he would be a fantastic lover, but I never imagined—

"Oh, damn that's my spot," I pant, digging my heels into his firm ass for leverage. He grunts in response, angling me a fraction lower on his sculpted forearms.

"It's mine now, Siah," he chuckles, as if I have revealed more of my secrets.

Anticipation mounts as he flexes powerful legs, working me up and down with practiced precision. Toned muscles cap his shoulders. My mouth waters as they grow slick from exertion.

"Yeah, do that again," I demand, locking my fingers around his neck. "Harder," I say, the word blunt and harsh, as I bounce my ass faster than a seasoned jockey on a thoroughbred in the final stretch.

And guess what? He doesn't leave me hanging.

The feel of his large hands holding me open as he thrusts deeper inside, drives me wild. Frantic and wet slapping sounds of my hips slamming down on his steely cock ricochet all around us.

"I could get loss in you forever, Siah akai," he rasps in my ear, the graveled sound of his voice heightening my senses.

He called me, my love. My breath hitches as my pulse quickens. A flush of heat spreads through my chest. I feel beads of perspiration forming in the valley between my breasts. The urge to give him more than my body grips me, but I clamp my lips tight.

This is a game, a voice warns. A reminder that even Dorothy had to leave Oz.

"You know this word, akai?"

On occasion I've heard him speak Japanese with his friends during a basketball game or in frustration, but this is the first time he's directed an endearment in his native language at me. Am I doing that thing when a one-night stand makes a moment into a marriage proposal? Nope. Not going there, not phoning there, not even sending a mother fucking text to that kind of trouble. Knox and I are friends.

Fucking friends.

He quiets, his ragged breathing evens as he waits for my answer. I can't. Then I remember my cautious inner self has had my vagina on a dusty shelf for half a decade. My performance deserves this man's praise. I know it's my pussy he loves, but it's been a minute since a man gave me something other than the brush off.

"I do," is all I say, and the simple phrase strikes a resounding cord. Drake and Deja's wedding brought us to Italy, but for me— this feels like a honeymoon.

I see this man-intense, tanned, inky strands damp with perspiration. I smell this man-dark, warm, spiced. I want this man, now and forever. I'd be a fool to surrender more than I have, so I tighten my legs around his waist, urging him on. He not only watches me with those midnight feline eyes, he listens. My moans, my sighs, my pauses—like a secret agent he decodes my body's language revealing my unspoken truth. Does my touch belie the years I've yearned for his possession? Can he hear the words my lips will never tell?

"Watashi no ai," he whispers before I hear, "forever."

This one I don't know the English translation, but the affection in his tone strokes across my heart with a lightness of a feather.

"What did say," I ask. As the hours have fallen away, the banter between us ebbs and flows from flirtatious to futuristic. This is the first time he's said forever. Two firsts in one night. Can I trust this love and the future he speaks? I want to believe so bad that my heart aches.

Knox slows his movements, yet he's reached deeper inside me. Our bodies are inseparable, fire and flame, burning as one.

"Feel my translation," his whispers.

And, I do. My heart wants to hold onto this soaring above the clouds feeling of being loved, writing a happy ending to our short story. Friends who touch one another with love, but can never be lovers. We have no future beyond these walls.

Right?

"I know you want to," I state boldly, relishing the ripple in the muscles across his broad back.

"Damn right," Knox growls as he tunnels deeper into my sex.

"That feels good," My inner thighs began to tremble; working to maintain a grip on his bucking hips.

"I'm not going anywhere, Siah."

He sounds so sure. Yet, certainty is the one thing I can not give. Either way, his words spur me on. I tighten my muscles, clamping my sex down on his pulsing rod. I hear the hitch in his breathing. I've got him in the palm of my hand.

He grips me harder, slamming that thick meat into my hungry center again and again. My breath comes in fragments and I swear spots cloud my vision. Maybe, I spoke too soon.

"Knox," I moan. The one word an admission that he has me too.

We're edging closer to oblivion, both of us grinding, grunting, straining sweaty limbs for another tumble into ecstasy.

I close my eyes, allowing each thrust of his rigid cock to ripple through me, the force is a seismic wave of vibration blurring every touch, every thought, every image until nothing exist beyond me...and this man. I coming, my velvet pussy—his description, not mine—milking his rod.

"Stay with me," he grunts, head flung back in a shuddering release.

"Yes," I whisper, in the heat of the moment.

My name is Siah Kent. The woman who lives her life through romantic heroines, book boyfriends, and my sex journal. Knox Ueno is mī fantajī, my fantasy wrapped in lean, hard muscle.

I should have stayed away because two days later I had to leave him.

End of Red Velvet Excerpt

Acknowledgement

I'd like to say an extra special thank you to Author Siera London for extending a warm invite into the Lunchtime Chronicle's world. I humbly appreciate her and the writing platform she has built and hope that it continues to spread joy to readers and inspiration to writers.

Thank you to my beta readers who dedicated their time to reading this book and providing top notch feedback. Afrikka Brooks Ennis, Zanthia Shaw-Matthews, and Lashonda Royal. You ladies are amazing. I cannot say thank you enough for your time and invaluable advice.

Author's Note

Readers, my sincere thank you for taking a chance on me and for choosing to read my first novella. Please leave a review letting me and others know what you thought of the book. If you enjoyed it or any of my other books, please pass them along to friends or anyone you think would enjoy them.

Other Titles by Keta Kendric

The Twisted Minds Series:

<u>Twisted Minds #1</u>
<u>Twisted Hearts #2</u>
<u>Twisted Secrets #3</u>
<u>Twisted Obsession #4</u>
<u>Twisted Revelation #5</u>
Twisted **Deception** – Coming 2021

The Chaos Series:

<u>Beautiful Chaos #1</u>
<u>Quiet Chaos #2</u>
<u>Hidden Chaos</u> – Coming 2021

Stand Alone:

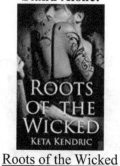

Roots of the Wicked

Novella:

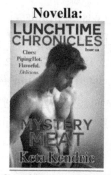

Coming 11.18.2020

Connect on Social Media

Subscribe to my Newsletter for exclusive updates on new releases, sneak peeks, deleted scenes, and much more. Join my Facebook Readers' Group, where you can live-chat about my books, enjoy contests, raffles, and giveaways.

Twitter:
https://twitter.com/AuthorKetaK

Instagram:
https://instagram.com/ketakendric

Pinterest:
https://www.pinterest.com/authorslist/

Bookbub:
https://www.bookbub.com/authors/keta-kendric

Newsletter:
https://mailchi.mp/c5ed185fd868/httpsmailchimp

Facebook Page:
https://www.facebook.com/AuthorKetaKendric

Goodreads:
https://www.goodreads.com/user/show/73387641-keta-kendric

Facebook Readers' Group:
https://www.facebook.com/groups/380642765697205/

Made in the USA
Middletown, DE
24 February 2024

49826500R00070